"**I** won't be able to give you what you need, Jack," Katrina said.

Jack didn't waste time on an answer but reached out to pull her against him. "I need you," he growled, his voice harsh with desire. He held her face close to his, his breath scorching her cheek. "Please . . . don't go."

She knew he would let her go if she wanted it. She met his eyes, rocked but not frightened by the devouring heat she saw in them. "I'll stay."

For a moment she wasn't sure he'd heard her. Then his mouth swooped down and captured her lips, kissing her so hard she forgot how to breathe. New feelings swelled inside her, pouring through her veins like rivers of sweet, crazy fire. She was burning out of control. If a kiss did this . . . "Jack, it's too fast. I can't—"

"Hush," he whispered. "I want you, Kitten. Only what you can give. Your laughter," he said, grazing her lips. "Your strength," he added, brushing his mouth over her bare shoulder. Then, looking into the velvet glory of her eyes, he said roughly, "And your heart. . . ."

WHAT ARE *LOVESWEPT* ROMANCES?

They are stories of true romance and touching emotion. We believe those two very important ingredients are constants in our highly sensual and very believable stories in the LOVESWEPT *line. Our goal is to give you, the reader, stories of consistently high quality that may sometimes make you laugh, sometimes make you cry, but are always fresh and creative and contain many delightful surprises within their pages.*

Most romance fans read an enormous number of books. Those they truly love, they keep. Others may be traded with friends and soon forgotten. We hope that each LOVESWEPT *romance will be a treasure—a "keeper." We will always try to publish*

LOVE STORIES YOU'LL NEVER FORGET
BY AUTHORS YOU'LL ALWAYS REMEMBER

The Editors

SMOOTH OPERATOR

RUTH
OWEN

BANTAM BOOKS
NEW YORK · TORONTO · LONDON · SYDNEY · AUCKLAND

SMOOTH OPERATOR
A Bantam Book / August 1993

ISBN 0-553-44265-1

Published simultaneously in the United States and Canada

Bantam Books are published by Bantam Books, a division of Bantam Dou-
bleday Dell Publishing Group, Inc. Its trademark, consisting of the words
"Bantam Books" and the portrayal of a rooster, is Registered in U.S. Patent
and Trademark Office and in other countries. Marca Registrada. Bantam
Books, 1540 Broadway, New York, New York 10036.

PRINTED IN THE UNITED STATES OF AMERICA

OPM   0 9 8 7 6 5 4 3 2 1

To Debbie Barr, Cynthia Powell, and especially Carol Quinto, for helping me to bring Einstein to life.

PROLOGUE

Katrina Sheffield pushed the blond fringe out of her eyes and glared in disbelief at the interoffice memo she held in her hands. "Chris," she muttered, "you're out of your tree. I know I asked for help, but . . . *Fagen*?"

She glanced over at the multiple stacks of paper on her desk, in the bins that could easily be labeled "Problems, problems, and more problems." As security manager of Sheffield Industries Miami Project Development Complex it seemed that all she did these days was specialize in problems. A month ago she'd asked her cousin Chris Sheffield, who headed up the development branch of their family business, to find her a reliable consultant to help restructure her security system. Three weeks ago Chris's wife Melanie had delivered their first child. Apparently fatherhood had scrambled his brain—normally Chris would never have suggested hiring someone as unacceptable as Jack Fagen to help her out.

Correction, she thought grimly. According to the memo, Fagen was already hired. She was supposed to meet with him tonight to discuss his assignment.

She'd sooner meet with the devil.

She stood up and paced her office in long-legged strides. "Fagen," she muttered angrily. "The man's strictly out for himself. He's an exploiter, an opportunist—"

"Actually," said a voice from the computer console in the corner of her office, "he's a Leo."

"Einstein?" Kat said, surprised to hear his voice. "I thought you were working on the weather projections for southeastern crop maximization."

"Did. Finished. Was piece of toast," Einstein said, using his favorite skewed expression. Einstein was Sheffield Industries' first artificial-intelligence computer. He could perform thousands of intricate calculations per minute, but the nuances of human speech occasionally eluded him. Hardly surprising, since he'd picked up most of his vocabulary from MTV and the Shopping Channel. "Besides," he added, cocking his video camera to one side, "this more interesting. Are we hiring 'the Terminator'?"

So even Einstein had heard of Jack Fagen's nickname. "Not if I can help it," she stated, angrily shaking her head. "The man is bad news. Maybe he is one of the best security consultants in the Western world, but he's got less human compassion than the machines he works on." Her violet eyes flashed with sudden and very real concern. "He could rip apart my entire 'neural net' if it doesn't meet his exacting standards. And lord knows what he'd do to PINK."

PINK, the Prototype for Intelligent Network Computers, was the joint creation of Einstein and the Sheffield technicians. She was the most advanced artificially generated intelligence in the world, but she had a nature as fickle as a firefly. PINK's frequent and highly dangerous travels over unsecured computer lines was the major source of Katrina's many headaches.

Einstein, however, didn't share Kat's concern over Fagen's influence on his protégée. His video camera spun three-sixty and his mechanical voice was modulated with laughter. "PINK'll drive him crazy. Be fun to watch."

"E, this is serious. Hiring Fagen would be an A-one security risk, worse than . . . than Preston Gates ever was." She cursed, hating the fact that she still stumbled over his name, even after all these months. "They're birds of a feather."

"Files indicate both are Caucasian males in their fourth decade of existence, employed in the computer industry," Einstein corrected. "Relation to avian species not documented."

"Sorry, my mistake," Kat said, mellowing somewhat at the computer's dedicated adherence to logic. Life would be a great deal simpler if she could live by figures and files, instead of the muddled, unreliable emotions that too often ruled her decisions. Figures and files . . .

She stopped pacing. "Einstein, can you get my secretary a complete listing of Jack Fagen's record by the end of the day?"

"Natch. Start right now," E said, signing off.

Katrina walked to her desk, a thoughtful smile playing on her lips. She studied Chris's memo, which included the address of the Coral Gables estate where Fagen was staying. It wasn't his own personal residence, she noted, since the memo stated he was installing a security system for the absent owner.

Not his address. Katrina leaned back in her chair and tapped her fingertips against her lips in concentration. As far as she could recall, Jack Fagen had no permanent address. He was a confirmed wanderer. That, in itself, seemed suspect.

Einstein's reliance on files and figures had given her an idea. Somewhere in Fagen's record there was bound to be an incident she could use to discredit him, something that would show Chris that Jack Fagen wasn't the kind of person they wanted working for Sheffield Industries. Chris might not put much faith in rumors, but Kat had learned the hard way that when it came to her system's security, it paid to be cautious. Besides, a man didn't get a nickname like Terminator by making friends and influencing people.

Terminator. Briefly she wondered why a man of his international reputation would take on the relatively small job of restructuring her security network. But then, why did a man like him do anything? She'd heard rumors that he was completely amoral, thoroughly unprincipled, and utterly ruthless.

She'd also heard rumors he was handsome as hell.

ONE

Jack Fagen had just settled into the armchair with a whiskey and the TV remote when the perimeter alarm light started flashing. "Not again," he groaned, casting his gaze skyward. "That's three times to-night. Can't that damn cat pick someone else's yard for a change?"

Fluffy, the neighbor's Persian, considered the garden his personal hunting ground, something Jack discovered only after he'd set up most of the minia-turized motion detectors and other surveillance equipment along the inside base of the perimeter wall. Today he'd gone back and reset the numerous, precisely calibrated, state-of-the-art detectors to ig-nore "Fluffy-sized" intruders. It was hot, painstak-ing work and it had left him in a foul mood. That mood hadn't improved when he discovered that he'd missed a few detectors. And when Fluffy managed to set off two of those missed detectors during the first quarter, Jack's mood took a nosedive.

It wasn't fair. All day long he'd been looking forward to indulging in one of the greatest pleasures the States had to offer a man—Monday-night football. But thanks to Fluffy he hadn't been able to watch five consecutive minutes of the game. For a short, gratifying moment he considered ignoring the third alarm. But years of Catholic-school training and army discipline had made honor and duty the watchwords of Jack's life. Responsibility was his middle name. Unfortunately.

Sighing, he clicked off the set and laid the remote down on the coffee table. He started to put down the tumbler, too, thought better of it, and downed the drink with a single, satisfying toss. Fluffy couldn't have it all his way, Jack decided.

He stood up, ran his fingers through his dark copper hair, and started his mental itinerary. Be quiet, be quick, be smart. Those three simple rules had saved his skin on more than one occasion. After all, he thought as he stepped through the French doors and onto the terrace, it might not be a cat. Odds were the intruder was Fluffy, but Jack's luck had a bad habit of running against the odds.

The night air blew sweet and cool against his face, stirring his hair and tickling his beard like a playful caress. He felt an ache deep inside him. His mind teased him with images of soft shoulders and hot kisses, and warm, compassionate eyes that promised more than brief, transitory pleasure.

Jack, you're losing it, he thought, shaking his head. This damn flower-stuffed garden was playing havoc with his libido. He stepped out into the garden, determined to fix the sensors, and possibly Fluffy, when he picked out a very uncatlike shape moving through the undergrowth.

Jack froze. Cursing under his breath, he realized he'd foolishly left his service revolver upstairs in his duffel bag. So much for being smart. He was just backing toward the house, wondering if he had time to call the police *and* retrieve his gun, when he simultaneously realized two things about the intruder. First, the would-be burglar was an amateur, since the movements lacked the deadly precision of the seasoned professional.

Second, it was a woman.

Scaling the wall was a breeze. Using the ancient vines as a ladder, Kat easily scrambled up the stone face and dropped to the soft ground on the other side with a single, muffled thump. The whole process took less than five minutes. "Piece of toast," she muttered, mimicking Einstein's slightly skewed expression.

She brushed a few stray leaves off her dark top, wishing she'd had something in her car trunk besides this salt-stiff, fishy-smelling windbreaker to cover her white blouse, or that she'd changed into a black shirt as well as black jeans for her after-hours interview with Jack Fagen. But then, she hadn't exactly dressed with housebreaking in mind. That had been a spur-of-the-moment idea.

Breaking and entering wasn't Katrina's favorite way to spend an evening. In fact, it rankled every fiber of her highly moral being. Still, she had no choice. She was desperate—desperate to find a way to keep the Terminator away from her computer system.

She'd spent the afternoon and early evening poring over the files Einstein had given to her secretary, Jenny. She scoured every page of the thick documents, searching for some plausible reason to not employ Fagen. And come up empty-handed. His official record was excellent, even incredible. After a brief tour of duty with the army's Special Services Branch, for which he'd been decorated, he'd gone into business for himself. Professionally she couldn't help but admire his results. He'd busted scams and industrial-espionage networks from New York to Hong Kong—nobody did it better. His client roster read like the Who's Who of the international computer industry, even including a few young democracies that he'd apparently waived his pricy fee to work for. Officially the Terminator was as clean as they come.

Which meant, she figured, that he was better at covering his tracks than she'd originally suspected. After all, Preston's credentials had seemed just as impressive, and look what a snake he'd turned out to be. Trusting by nature, Kat had learned the hard way that it paid to be suspicious, especially where handsome men with vaguely dubious reputations were concerned.

Which is why she'd embarked on a career of breaking and entering. As she'd driven past the ancient, vine-choked wall that surrounded the estate, she'd noticed a decided lack of security measures. She'd pulled to the side of the narrow, deserted road and cautiously stepped out for a closer look. What she'd seen had confirmed her suspicions. A child could have climbed that decaying wall, yet there were no floodlights, no surveillance cameras, and no electric eyes. In fact, except for a small camera perched above the estate's ornate ironwork gate, there didn't seem to be any kind of protection at all.

Jack Fagen's mystique dissolved like smoke in the wind. She realized she'd been in awe of the man, impressed by his legendary reputation. Even—yes, she could admit it now—even a little frightened at the thought of meeting him. But Fagen's skills had been vastly overrated. No security consultant worth his salt would design a system that monitored a reinforced gate and left easily scaled walls unprotected. Fagen was strictly bush league.

All she had to do now was prove it.

She squared her shoulders, looking around at the thick, overgrown garden she'd landed in. It was sadly neglected—apparently Fagen's house-sitting duties did not extend to the grounds. Ahead, she could make out the lights of the house through the dense greenery, a lone beacon cutting through the deep, oppressive night. Here, nature had reclaimed some of its own. Flowers spilled across the ground like fragrant, mystical carpets. Ancient live oaks towered above her, Spanish moss hanging limply from their branches like tangled witch's hair. Feelings strange and sensual stirred within Katrina, moving through her like a dark, hungry sea. Unsettled, she quickly thrust them aside.

She took a deep breath of the night air, ignoring the lush perfume of the flowers and concentrating instead on the jarring, head-clearing smell of the slightly fishy windbreaker. Fanciful thoughts were the last thing she needed. She wanted her wits sharp when she strolled oh-so-casually through the front door and watched Jack Fagen wipe the proverbial egg off his face.

⬥━━━━━⬥

A woman burglar, Jack thought, his mouth set in a grim line. And an amateur! He hated amateurs. They were twice as dangerous as professionals because they were three times as stupid. Jack advanced cautiously, wondering how the hell to deal with this situation. If it were a man, he'd just sneak up behind him and drop him with a quick shoulder chop. But a woman . . . The first thing Sister Barbara had drilled into him was never to hit a woman. Catholic-school habits died hard.

Jack was still trying to decide what to do when the woman intruder stopped. She looked around, though not in Jack's direction, then pushed back the concealing hood from her face. And Jack forgot all about Sister B, and manners, and even about amateur burglars.

"Mother of God," he breathed. Moonlight caressed the rich perfection of the intruder's skin and touched her halo hair with silver fire. And that face . . . that face could drive a man crazy. Startled, he stepped back. A branch broke under his foot, sounding like a gunshot to his ears. Luckily the beauty didn't seem to notice.

He moved closer, wanting a closer look at her face. Or maybe he just wanted to see if she was real. He'd dreamed of a woman like her for so long, he wasn't sure if he was dreaming still. But she seemed real. She looked real. He stepped closer, near enough to touch her, near enough to catch her scent. What did perfection smell like? he wondered. He took a deep breath of the flower-heavy air and caught the odor of . . . fish?

Katrina pushed aside the larger branches and walked toward the light from the house, concentrating on making her steps as silent as possible. But her concentration wavered.

The night world closed around her, hushed and full of secret shadows. Small animals skittered through the underbrush, and night birds called plaintively in the distance. The exotic, sensual feelings she'd experienced before returned with a vengeance, touching something deep and wild in her heart, something primitive. Leaves brushed by her as she passed, stroking her with a lover's intimacy. She felt strangely hot, oddly disoriented—as if a stranger had slipped beneath her skin.

The air hung thick with the scents of honeysuckle and lilac. Mesmerized, she pushed back the fishy-smelling hood of her windbreaker and drank deeply of the sweet night air. It poured through her like a tonic, making every inch of her body feel vital and alive. Restless passions stirred within her, like an animal kept too long behind bars—

A branch snapped. Old thoughts and feelings returned in a rush, leaving her confused and oddly disappointed. She didn't dwell on the feelings. She didn't have time. Something was out there watching her, something large enough to break a fairly good-sized branch. Something . . . or someone.

Rats, I've probably been spotted. Grimly she realized that Jack Fagen's security system worked pretty well after all. Her plan had backfired, badly. Too late she saw what a ridiculous position her little stunt had placed her in. She was going to come out of this looking like a complete fool, unless . . .

She paused, pretending once more to be entranced by the beauty of the night. Ears attuned, she heard the unseen watcher move nearer and nearer, until there was hardly a yard between them. She willed herself to wait . . . wait. Then, with all her strength she struck out, pushing through the screen of leaves and branches with all her might. A muffled "umph" informed her that she'd connected with some part of the man's anatomy, but she didn't wait around to find out exactly which part. She turned on her heels and ran toward the distant wall as if Satan himself were after her.

She was quick, but Jack was quicker. He dove and caught her legs, pitching them both into the thick undergrowth. Crying out, she struggled to get free, fighting like a wildcat against his greater strength. In the end strength won.

"You're good," he acknowledged, looking down at her tight, defiant face. "But I'm better."

"Go to hell," she said.

Jack smiled. No hysterics, no pleading for mercy. He liked that. "Be glad to, sweetheart. Just as soon as you tell me who you are, and what you're doing here."

She didn't answer. A band of moonlight fell across her face, illuminating her bright, impossibly large eyes. Hate-filled eyes. *Lord, she's got nerve*, he thought, impressed. She was frightened, he could tell by the erratic heartbeat that hammered so close to his own. But frightened as she was, she wasn't going to give him an inch. Not a single inch.

Still, this wasn't getting him anywhere. He couldn't stay here all night on top of her—pleasant as that notion might be. "Listen," he told her. "We can do this the easy way or the hard way. Your choice."

"I'm not saying anything," she hissed, "not until you let me—hey, what are you doing?"

"The hard way," he answered as he ran his free hand deftly down her body, searching for some ID.

"Stop. You can't—" Her words ended in an abrupt gasp as Jack searched a strategic part of her abdomen. By the time she recovered, he'd already found what he was looking for. Her windbreaker pocket yielded an old battered sales receipt. He held it up to the moonlight and had no trouble at all making out the bold, neat signature.

"What the . . . ?" Jack began, looking down at the now quiet woman. Her silence, combined with her glum expression, told him everything he needed to know. He sat back on his heels and laughed genuinely for the first time in months. "Damn pleased to meet you—boss!"

Kat walked across the terrace and into the living room, trying to look more composed than she felt. She wished fervently for a rock large enough to crawl under—though she'd settle for one large enough to deck Jack Fagen with. The man was worse than even she'd expected. He had no business searching her like that, touching her that . . . intimately. Embarrassed heat spread through her at the memory of his hands on her body—sure, practiced hands that drew liquid fire across her skin, arousing her in spite of herself. She'd never felt such heat, and hated the fact that it was Jack Fagen who'd made her feel it. *Search*, *my eye*, she thought angrily. The bastard was copping a quick one.

"Can I get you anything?"

Great, now *he remembers his manners*, Kat

thought, fuming. She turned around, ready to give Fagen her unabridged opinion of his etiquette. The words died on her tongue.

Jack Fagen was built like a mountain, strong and imposing, with muscles that looked like they'd been chiseled from granite. She hadn't been aware of it while they were in the garden, but inside, his size dwarfed even this spacious living room. His shaggy, copper-colored hair and full beard suited his rugged features, and his eyes held the wide blue of the open sky. Katrina swallowed, suddenly unbalanced. Standing near him made her feel slight and vulnerable—a new experience for a woman who had to look down to meet the eyes of most of the men she knew.

"Can I get something for you, Ms. Sheffield?" he repeated.

Blinking, she remembered who he was. Fagen the opportunist. Fagen the unscrupulous. She straightened her shoulders and stated, "You've done quite enough already, Mr. Fagen. You had no reason to . . . manhandle me like that."

Jack could think of several reasons right off, though he doubted she was in the mood to appreciate them. Not now, anyway. He searched through the reasons and settled on the least interesting one. "Well, you might have been armed. You could've been carrying a concealed weapon."

"Not in the places you searched," she quipped.

Jack smiled—a slow, devilish smile that made her stomach do a somersault. "I don't know," he mused. "I once knew this woman in Bangkok who—"

"Never mind," Kat interrupted, paling at the thought of Fagen describing the various uses of the female anatomy.

Jack's smile turned into a grin. He liked this woman. He liked her intriguing mix of steel nerves and flustered innocence. He liked her body too. Even wearing that shapeless windbreaker, she was, he could see, tall and slender, and his recent search had assured him that she was rounded in all the right places. "What were you doing out there, anyway?"

"I wanted to talk with you—"

He gave her a sharp, incredulous look. "So why not use the phone? Or ring the front door bell?"

Kat stiffened. "All right," she admitted. "I was testing your security system. I wanted to see if you're as good as they say you are."

Jack leaned against the back of an armchair, watching her intently. "And am I?" he asked softly.

He wasn't talking about the system and Katrina knew it. Again she remembered the feel of his hands on her, the unwelcome, yet undeniable heat of his touch. She closed her eyes, hoping that blocking out the sight of his rakishly handsome face would clear her head. It did . . . a little.

She opened her eyes. "Mr. Fagen, I—"

"Jack," he interrupted. "Under the circumstances I think we can skip the formalities."

Katrina recalled the "circumstances" and swallowed. "Look, Mr. Fa—okay, Jack—I think it's only fair to tell you that . . . well, I'm not sure you'd be interested in working at Sheffield. It wouldn't be as exciting as the jobs you're used to."

Jack recalled the flashing violet eyes and the playmate curves hidden beneath the concealing windbreaker. Personally he thought working with this woman would be plenty exciting. "Nice of you to be so concerned for my welfare, Katrina, but I'm sure—"

"Kat," she corrected. "People call me Kat."

"Why not Katrina?"

"Because I don't like it." *Because the only one who ever called me by that name was Preston.* Once again she squared her shoulders. "Look, Jack, let me give it to you straight. I'm not sure I want you working with me."

She expected some kind of reaction—anger, a violent rebuke, something. Instead the edge of his mouth turned up in a disarming grin and she caught the glint of humor in his sky-blue eyes. "Oh? Why not, Katrina?"

"Kat!" she stated, thrown off balance by his composure. "Look, I'll make sure you're compensated for any inconvenience. Don't worry about the money—"

"I never worry about money," he said with a frankness that made her believe him. "Everything I own in the world is packed in a duffel bag upstairs. I work the jobs that interest me. And frankly working with you interests me a great deal."

He's talking about the security system. Please make him be talking about the security system, thought Kat. The room felt hotter. Jack hadn't moved, he still leaned on the back of the armchair facing her, but she had the most uncanny sensation that he'd just come across the room to stand beside her. A breeze blew through the French doors, filling the room with the heavy fragrance of the garden. Her body quickened at the scent, and she could tell by the subtle tensing in Jack's shoulders that he was react-ing to it too.

What was happening to her? True, it'd been almost a year since she'd been with Preston, but surely she wasn't desperate enough to take a roll on the carpet with a complete stranger. Even if that stranger did have a body to die for and the bluest eyes she'd ever seen . . .

She tore her gaze away. "This isn't going to work out. This just isn't going to work out."

This time her words did make an impression on him. He walked around the armchair and came over to her, moving with the smooth determination of a well-oiled machine. Katrina's heart pounded so hard, she was sure he could hear it. There was no mistaking the look in his eyes. Predatory. Hungry. Like a tiger about to strike. Or a man about to—

"You know what I think?" he said softly as he reached her. "I think you're afraid."

Kat tried to laugh, but it came out as more of a gasp. Jack's nearness was making it unaccountably difficult to breathe. "Afraid?" she said, trying to keep her voice light and level. "I'm not afraid of anything."

Jack shook his head, his eyes fixed on hers. "Lying doesn't become you, Katrina."

"Kat," she said weakly. He stood a foot away from her, not touching her. He didn't have to. The man set up a chain reaction through her system, causing tiny, delicious explosions though her entire body.

Jack's smile deepened. His gaze left her eyes to focus on her lips, and . . . lower. "I don't think you think you can handle me."

Anger pricked at her, lending her strength. She took a step back and raised her chin. "I could handle you with one hand tied behind my back."

"Intriguing idea," Jack returned. "If you're into that sort of thing."

"Don't mock me," she said, using her anger as a

shield. "If we do work together, it will be as business associates, nothing more. And I don't think you can handle that!"

The flash of surprise in his eyes told her that she'd hit close to the mark, much closer than she'd expected. All at once she sensed the emptiness in him, the weariness of a man who's spent too much of his life fighting battles. Ashamed, she realized she'd just given him another.

She wanted to believe his vulnerability was real, not some ploy he used on women to get his own way. She wanted to believe a human heart beat beneath his smooth, polished exterior. His eyes captured hers, holding her prisoner as his hands had held her prisoner in the garden. Truth was in those eyes, and strength enough to build a lifetime on. *Eyes don't lie*, whispered an inner voice.

And there's a sucker born every minute, whispered another.

Kat turned away, amazed and a little disgusted at the naïveté of her thoughts. This was the Terminator, the man whose motto was "the end justified the means." He was using her, as he used everyone else in his life. Well, two could play at that game. "You're good, Fagen. And because you're good I'll work with you, because my system deserves the best. But," she continued, looking back at him, "you make one false move, or use any of your famous commando tactics on my system, and I'll make you regret you were ever born. Okay?"

Jack's powerful bearing spoke of a man who liked to make his own rules, not have them made for him. For a moment Kat wondered if he'd accept her terms, and was surprised to realize she truly wanted him to. Then he ran his hand through his hair and sighed with something that sounded like resignation. "Deal," he said simply.

The bargain struck, Katrina left the house and stepped into the night, hoping its velvet darkness would soothe her jangled nerves. No such luck. The more she tried not to think of Jack, the more his image came into her mind, spinning her senses like a child's top. Try as she might, she couldn't forget the haunting vulnerability she'd glimpsed in his eyes, any more than she could forget the crazy heat that melted through her every time his blue eyes met hers. Nor, she realized with a shock, did she really want to.

Jack looked after her, watching her walk down the long driveway and disappear into the deep shadows of the night. The soft disappointment he'd kept hidden during their conversation crept into his eyes. *Katrina*, he thought, with mixed emotions. For a moment he'd thought he'd glimpsed something special behind those violet eyes, a strength of character he'd encountered only once or twice before in all his travels. But it had only been bad temper. The woman had more bristles than a porcupine, and Jack had better things to do with his time than pull out her barbs.

Still, she had by far the sexiest body he'd ever seen. Those hot, heady moments in the garden had set his personal security system to "Defcon 2," one step away from outright attack. He'd never experienced such an immediate, overwhelming attraction to a woman, and from her hasty exit he was pretty sure she'd felt it too. Her prickly personality didn't thrill him, but Jack had learned the hard way not to expect too much from any relationship. Sister Barbara may have raised him on the ideals of love and devotion—reality had taught him different lessons.

He breathed in the night air, clearing his mind of memories and lost dreams. Reality had its own rewards. And, realistically speaking, it would be better if he didn't particularly want to get to know Katrina Sheffield. He couldn't afford to get personally involved with her.

That could blow his major objective all to hell.

TWO

Katrina arrived fifteen minutes late for work the next morning, blaming her tardiness on bad traffic, and overlooking the fact that she'd changed outfits three times before deciding on a simple white linen suit and a royal-blue silk blouse. She wanted to look her best for Jack Fagen—her *professional* best, of course. Last night she'd imagined herself attracted to him. The moonlight, the garden, the strange, haunted quality of the night . . . all had combined to make her see him as some devastating mystery man, utterly irresistible.

Poppycock, she thought as she slipped her key card into the automatic reader. Daylight would evaporate those night dreams. She'd see that Jack was just as ordinary as every other man she knew—and she wondered why she wasn't more pleased by the thought.

The harsh buzzer startled her out of her imaginings. She pushed open the heavy door, wondering why someone couldn't invent a pleasant way to indicate that a security card had been logged and accepted. Apparently obnoxious security buzzers were as much a part of her profession as, well, obnoxious security consultants.

Kat's first stop was usually the computer lab, where she checked with Leonard or one of the other analysts to see how PINK was doing. But this morning she turned away from the lab and headed down the hallway toward Jenny's desk, intending to warn her efficient but impressionable young secretary that Fagen would be arriving any minute. Jenny wasn't there. Katrina frowned. It wasn't like Jenny to be late, and the girl never left her desk without first asking someone to cover for her. Where could she be?

Suddenly Katrina's attention was drawn to her office by a high-pitched giggle coming through the half-open door. "Oh, Mr. Fagen!"

Jenny. Jenny was in Katrina's office—and so, apparently, was Jack. The laughter grated on Katrina's nerves like sandpaper. "Swell," she grumbled as she walked purposefully toward the door. "He's here fifteen minutes and he's already making time with my secretary. Well, if he thinks I'll stand for that, he's in for a—"

Katrina stopped midsentence. She caught sight of Jack, sitting casually on the edge of her office desk, his mountainous form making the substantial piece of furniture look like a Tinkertoy. His gray suit was cut in the European style, suggesting the strength of his body rather than flaunting it. Memories of last night jolted through her like an electric shock. She gripped the doorknob to support her suddenly unsteady legs. Fagen in a sweatshirt and jeans had overwhelmed her. Fagen in a tailored suit devastated her. He was that rare kind of man who would look good in whatever he wore. And better in nothing at all.

Neither of the office's occupants had noticed Kat. Jenny still twittered, and Fagen gave her a winning smile. "None of this 'Mr. Fagen' stuff, okay? It makes me feel like I'm back in parochial school."

Reform school is more like it, thought Kat sourly. She pushed open the door and stepped boldly into the office. "Good morning, Jenny. I see you've already met *Mr. Fagen*."

Jack turned to face her, his smile transforming into a deeper, richer expression. "Good morning to you, Ms. Sheffield. I didn't expect to beat you in this morning. But then, you did leave my place rather late last night. . . ."

Jenny swung around to face Katrina, her eyes wide with interest.

"We had a meeting," Kat said, realizing too late that her blurted-out explanation was more damning than silence. She gave Jack a warning look. "A *business* meeting."

"Of course," Jack said, but his look said different. Desire smoldered in his eyes, licking her skin like a hot blue flame. Heat exploded in exquisitely inconvenient places, shocking and arousing her at once. Instinctively her body gave in to the yearning . . . until she heard the soft click of her office door closing. Jenny had slipped out of the room, no doubt believing that her boss and Jack wanted to be alone.

"Lord," she groaned, casting her eyes skyward. "She probably thinks something happened between us."

"Didn't it?" Jack asked, smiling broadly.

His grin had a predatory cast to it, displaying his even, sinister-looking white teeth. Kat had a quick vision of an enormous, copper-furred wolf licking his lips as he watched defenseless Red Riding Hood. She gasped, but not entirely from fear. Honestly, the man should come with a warning label. "Look," she said, her temper rising. "Nothing happened between us, and I don't appreciate you making people think it did. Especially not Jenny. She knows you and I just met yesterday and I don't want her thinking . . . well, she's an impressionable young girl—"

"Right, and you're old enough to be talking like her mother," said Jack as he rose from the desk. "What are you? Thirty-three? Thirty-four?"

"Twenty-eight!" Kat sputtered. Too late she saw the gleam of humor in his blue eyes and realized he'd been teasing her.

"I would have guessed twenty-five, Katrina," he said, his smile softening.

She wanted to dislike him. Lord, how she wanted to. But how could she when he spoke her name like that? Katrina. The name curled through her, tantalizing, full of promises that made her body quiver. No woman on earth could resist that soft, sweet invitation. But she had to resist it. Her instincts warned her that despite his winning charm and impeccable record, Jack Fagen was not to be trusted. He was hiding something—she'd have bet money on it. Her last liaison with a questionable character had all but destroyed her professional credibility, and nearly broken her heart.

Once bitten, twice shy. She turned her back to him and walked to the door. "We'd better get to work," she said, keeping her voice level and noncommittal. "I thought we'd start with a tour of the security facilities, then meet with the prototypes.

And, by the way, I'd prefer it if you didn't call me Katrina."

Jack followed her. She felt him behind her, tall and overwhelming, undeniably male. He stood so close, she could catch the spice scent of his after-shave, feel his warm breath on her hair. Her whole body pulled taut. *Don't let him touch me*, she prayed. *I'll lose it completely if he touches me.*

He didn't touch her. Instead he moved away. When she turned around, she caught him studying her with an intense, oddly uncertain expression. "You are one tough lady to figure out. But I'll make a bargain with you. I won't call you Katrina if you won't call me Mr. Fagen. Deal?"

Katrina's tension left in a rush. "Deal," she told him, once more assuming the role of the competent corporate executive. They'd just reached a compromise. Maybe this partnership would work out after all. Now, if she could just stop visualizing herself in a red hood . . .

They spent the rest of the morning touring the development facility, meeting the personnel, and generally letting Jack get familiar with the various systems. Jack studied the equipment, but as often as not he found himself studying Katrina as well. He liked the way she handled her staff, firm but fair, with a ready concern for all their questions and comments. Her security systems and procedures were also top of the line. Jack had seen larger systems than Katrina's, but rarely one as well run. He was impressed.

Other things impressed him, too, like the way her trim figure filled out the classic white suit she wore. Her movements were strong and sure, but with a womanly grace that filled Jack's mind with very unprofessional thoughts. He wondered what she'd say if she knew that instead of concentrating on the security schematics she'd provided, he was secretly studying her calves. Probably nothing printable, he imagined, smiling.

"What's so funny?"

Jack looked up, startled that she'd been watching him close enough to catch his slight smile. The lady didn't miss much. "I was thinking how unusual it is to find such a remarkable facility, and with such a remarkable woman at the helm."

He'd meant the compliment sincerely, but instead of being pleased, she bristled. He could almost see her hackles rising. "I'm glad you like my system, because I respect your opinion as a trained professional. As for your opinion of me," she added, shrugging, "you should consider me just another piece of equipment."

Jack's smile deepened into a wolfish grin. "Does

that mean I get to inspect you like I inspected all the other equipment?"

Kat's temper sparked. "I'll tell you what you can do with your inspecting—" she began in what promised to be a colorful tirade, but she stopped when one of her analysts knocked on the office door and entered the room.

"Sorry to interrupt you, Ms. Sheffield."

"Oh, yes, Leonard," she said, waving the thin man into the room. "Is anything wrong?"

"No, no. I just came to tell you Einstein's finished with the ozone calculations. I've put him online, so you can talk with him through your console."

"Thanks," said Kat, impressed as always by Leonard's thoughtfulness. Certain people could take lessons. "Jack, this is Leonard Heep, my senior technical analyst. And my unofficial assistant. If you want to know something about our system hardware, he's your man."

Jack gave the narrow-faced man a searching look, then held out his hand. "It sounds like Ms. Sheffield thinks quite highly of your abilities. That's a real compliment coming from her."

Leonard's thin palm met Jack's robust one in a perfunctory shake. "Yes, I have the utmost respect for *Ms. Sheffield*," he said, giving a subtle but distinct

emphasis to her name. He turned back to Katrina.
"Do you need me to do anything else?"

"No, not right now. And thank you."

Leonard scurried out of the room. Jack looked
after him, a wry smile on his lips. He'd gotten the
same cool greeting from several of the other programmers, a sort of "Yankee go home," computer
style. It was a safe bet he wasn't going to win any
popularity contests with Katrina or her employees.
He stole a quick, furtive look at her long, shapely
legs. *Damn shame*.

Without waiting for an invitation, he walked
over and pulled a chair up to the console beside
Katrina. "Nice guy, that Heep, but I don't think he's
crazy about me being here."

That makes two of us, she thought glumly. "Leonard's just concerned about the system. He's put
almost as much time into building it as I have. He's
totally dedicated to his work, and he's the best as-
sembler programmer I know. He reads core dumps
like some people read comic books."

"There's more to life than core dumps, Kat,"
Jack said softly. "For everyone."

His voice stroked her senses like silk, smooth and
exquisitely provocative. Lord, he rattled her, but she
wasn't about to let him know that. She concentrated
on typing in the series of access commands that
would down-link Einstein to her terminal. That

accomplished, she checked the wires on the compact speaker, adjusted the video camera, and pulled the flexible microphone toward her. "Einstein, there's someone here who wants to meet you."

The video camera whirred and focused on Jack. "Terminator!" cried Einstein without waiting for formal introductions. "What's shakin'?"

Jack laughed at Einstein's enthusiastic response. "I see my reputation precedes me."

"Affirmative, dude. Nineteen eighty-nine—busted the Berlin Conspiracy; 1990—disabled the Singapore–London Smuggling Network; 1991—set up Kuwait City resistance communication network during Desert Storm; 1992—"

"You were in Kuwait City during the war?" asked Kat, surprise making her forget her dislike.

"Well, yes," admitted Jack, "though the mission was supposed to be classified. How did you find out about it, Einstein?"

"I'll never tell."

Jack's flashing blue eyes met Kat's in a devilish wink. "He's got a mind of his own, hasn't he?"

So, apparently, had Jack. Katrina had trouble reconciling the image of the self-serving opportunist with a freedom fighter, putting his life on the line to aid the beleaguered citizens of Kuwait. She'd seen pictures, heard stories of the terrible price many resistance workers paid for their patriotism. They must have paid him a great deal for his services. Yes, that was it. He must have done it for the money. . . .

"Kat, is something wrong with that dial?"

Kat looked down, realizing that she'd spent the last few minutes adjusting the color on Einstein's monitor, which was now a dramatic shade of fuchsia. That would teach her to let her mind wander. "There was," she said, forcing a smile, "but I fixed it."

Einstein's camera swiveled and focused on the dial. "Explain how fuchsia fixes."

Mind your own beeswax, E, she thought. Aloud, she said, "Later. Right now I'd like you to get PINK so we can—"

"Pink what?" Jack questioned.

"Not what. Who," Kat explained. "Prototype for Intelligent Network Computers. We call her PINK for short."

"And cause she likes it," added Einstein.

"And because she likes it," Kat admitted, smiling. It was hard not to smile when she thought of the independent little computer. "Get her for us, will you, E?"

"Well . . ."

Katrina's smile disappeared. "Don't tell me she's broken out again."

"Okay. I won't."

Kat groaned. "E, get her back. Now."

"She's not gonna like it."

Kat grabbed the microphone. "I don't give a—Einstein, it's dangerous for her out there. You know what unshielded system hopping exposes her to. Get her back. Tell her . . . tell her if she's not back in two hours, I'll disconnect her cable-TV connection for a month. You know what that means."

E moaned. "No MTV. No 'Wheel of Fortune.' And no . . ." he added, lowering his voice to a horrified whisper, "no Shopping Channel."

"That's right," Kat said. "I'm sorry to be so harsh, but it's the only way she's going to learn. Please go get her."

The light winked out on Einstein's video camera, indicating that he'd done just that. Katrina leaned back in her chair and pressed her hands against her aching temples. *Why me, Lord?* she thought. *Why—*

"Ahem."

Jack. Oh, damn, she'd forgotten about him. He'd heard the whole thing, and seen firsthand how easily PINK breached her security system. She'd put her lifeblood into building this system. She was proud of it, and she wanted Jack to be as proud of it as she was. No chance of that now. "Well, now you know," she said, not daring to look at him. "My security system is about as 'secure' as Swiss cheese.

The more system holes I plug, the more PINK opens. It's hopeless. I'll . . . I'll understand if you don't want to take on a losing proposition."

For a long moment Jack was silent. Then he said, "Are you still trying to get rid of me, Kat?"

"No," she said quickly, and realized that she meant it. She turned slowly to face him. "No," she repeated, this time with conviction. "Actually I'd appreciate your help."

"Then you've got it," Jack said, meeting her gaze. She had, he decided, the most incredible eyes. They could change from ice to fire in a moment, from deep blue to flashing violet. And sometimes, like now, they contained an indigo softness that drew him like a spell. Suddenly he was back in the garden, in the dark and the heat and the sweetness, holding her body under his. Only this time she wasn't fighting.

Desire lashed him like a whip. He shuddered, surprised and unnerved by the intensity of the feeling. Liking the lady was one thing, but this—this feeling rocked him to his core. He wasn't sure what it was. He wasn't sure he wanted to know. He coughed, covering his confusion. "It's hot in here. I need some air."

Kat looked at her watch. "Okay. It's just about noon. We could break for lunch. The company cafeteria is just down the hallway—"

"No. Outside." Jack got up from his chair. "Someplace where a man can breathe."

"All right," Kat said, rising also. "There's a restaurant on the boardwalk, near the beach."

"Fine." He hurried out of her office.

Kat followed him down the hallway, puzzled by his abrupt departure. But then, many things about Jack Fagen puzzled her. Like a multilevel security program, the more she uncovered, the more complicated he appeared to be. Who was he really? she wondered.

And why did she care?

"I'll get it."

"No, I'll get it."

"I'll get it," Katrina repeated, reaching for the lunch check. "I'm the boss."

"But I'm the guy," said Jack. He deftly scooped up the check and headed for the front register, ignoring her protests.

Not that this stopped her. "That," she said as she caught up with him, "is the dumbest, most outdated comment I've heard this year. It's practically prehistoric."

"Yeah," Jack answered, smiling. "But I'm a prehistoric kind of guy."

Kat paled. Images of Jack as a primitive caveman

assaulted her mind, making her feel extremely foolish, and extremely aroused, all at once. Luckily Jack was paying the check and had his back to her. Unluckily she found herself studying his broad shoulders and tapered waist, and tried not to picture him in a loincloth.

Outside on the boardwalk the bright sunshine and the ocean breeze helped restore her equilibrium. Scattered whitecaps winked across the blue surface, and waves rolled onto the shore with unhurried grace. Katrina closed her eyes and took a deep breath of the fresh salt air, remembering the happy days she'd spent with her family at the beach.

"Lord, watch over me, for the sea is so vast and my boat is so small," Jack said softly, just behind her.

Kat opened her eyes and looked at him, surprised by both his words and the softness of his tone. He stared out at the water, oddly expressionless, but something in the set of his jaw reminded her of the deep, aching sadness she'd sensed in him last night.

He continued, speaking almost more to himself than to her. "I learned that before I ever saw an ocean, when the largest body of water I knew was the sunken underpass beneath the Loop after a heavy rain. One of the nuns at school taught it to me."

"Nuns?" she said incredulously.

Jack's mouth softened into a smile. "Don't knock it. Sister Barbara was tougher than any drill sergeant

I had in the army. She never let me get away with anything—at least not the stuff she knew about. She rode me ragged. But she was always there when I needed her. She even got me out of Juvey Hall a couple of times when my mother couldn't be bothered."

He spoke the damning statement so casually that at first Katrina thought she'd misunderstood him. Her family's love defined her life. As a gawky, too-tall youngster, she'd found instant acceptance among the rough-and-tumble wolf pack of Sheffield cousins. As a young teen grieving over her mother's death, she'd found the love and sympathy she'd needed to get past the pain. And as Preston's tainted pawn, she'd found unwavering support, and a belief in her innocence that far exceeded her own.

She couldn't imagine existing without the anchoring love of a family. But, apparently, that was the reality of Jack's early years. She didn't know which horrified her more: his mother's indifference, or his casual acceptance of the fact. "What about your father?"

"What about him?" said Jack, shrugging. He continued to look at the sea, keeping his thoughts to himself. The wind had blown a strand of copper hair across his cheek, and she desperately wanted to reach up and smooth it back in place. She stopped herself, barely. She felt vulnerable and confused. Compassion for the boy and suspicion of the man warred within her, threatening to breach her own carefully constructed internal security system.

As if sensing her confusion, Jack turned to her, searching her with his intense, unbelievably sexy eyes. She felt naked, as if those eyes could see straight into her secret heart. Then, suddenly, that intensity vanished. His eyes took on a hard glint, like cold, tempered steel. "Don't take me too seriously, Kat. That was the orphan-boy scenario."

"Orphan boy?" she echoed.

"My canned speech about my past. I have a dozen to choose from. Orphan boy, rich man's illegitimate son, military brat. I tell the one that gets me the farthest," he said grimly. He looked into her with his harsh, unyielding eyes. "That's who I am."

Katrina should have been furious. But a lifetime spent in the company of her male cousins had taught her that there were lies and lies. Some men told lies to protect themselves, others told lies to protect others. Instinct deeper than reason told her that Jack's lie was the second kind. She felt she'd caught a brief glimpse of the real Jack Fagen, and the knowledge made her laugh out loud. "You may be a scoundrel, Jack Fagen, but at least you're an honest one."

And, to her surprise, the coldhearted security consultant began laughing too.

————————⟐————————

"Shopping Channel," Jack said as he opened the passenger door.

Katrina got out. "What about it?" she asked as she smoothed her skirt.

Jack made a concerted effort to keep his mind off her endless legs, and was at least partially successful. "The Shopping Channel," he said as they walked across the grassy mall toward the Sheffield building. "Einstein made a big deal about it when he was talking about PINK. Why?"

Business as usual, Kat thought with a twinge of regret. She'd begun to enjoy their newfound camaraderie, not to mention the pleasant warmth that seeped through her as she sat next to him in the car. Sighing, she answered, "There's an anomaly in E's programming. He's a shopaholic."

"Shopaholic?" Jack said, fighting a grin.

"It's not funny," she scolded, though she, too, was having trouble keeping a straight face. "He's a terrible impulse buyer. Put the word 'sale' on it, and he buys it. My cousin's wife Melanie—she's Einstein's inventor—tried her best to find the bug, but it seems to be an intrinsic part of his programming."

"Now I've heard everything."

"Don't count on it," she said wryly. "E's anomaly was replicated in PINK's programming, with one slight twist. Instead of buying things, she . . . buys chances."

"Chances? You mean she gambles?"

"On anything and everything," Kat admitted sadly. "That's why she keeps breaking out, to place bets. She thinks it's fun, but it's a major headache for me. Hialeah Park Racetrack is about to sue us for wreaking havoc with their accounting system. And you should have heard the language the lottery official used when I told him she'd reprogrammed the state's lotto computer to pick her numbers—"

"You were right," said Jack, nodding. "I hadn't heard everything. Well, if your only security exposure is a gambling computer, I don't think you've got too much to worry about."

But Kat knew it wasn't her only exposure, at least historically. Last year she'd narrowly thwarted a major security crime, a crime for which she was partly responsible, whatever her cousin said. As her associate, Jack had a right to know the facts. She took a deep, steadying breath and began to tell him about Preston.

"About a year ago Sheffield security was breached. An embezzlement ring used the core mainframe computer to break into the pension systems of several major corporations. They reactivated the accounts of deceased members, but had the checks sent to themselves."

"Zombies," Jack commented. "The living dead. 'Zombie' embezzlement was fairly common in the early days of computing, but today's sophisticated electronic auditing procedures make it practically impossible. I'm surprised they got away with it."

You weren't the only one, she thought bitterly. She continued her story, pleased that despite her inner turmoil, her voice remained confident and professional. Maybe she was beginning to get this thing out of her system after all. "Sheffield's powerful mainframe allowed them to override the auditing procedures. And the remote access node allowed them a backdoor into the pension systems, a completely untraceable backdoor."

Jack gave a low whistle. "Quite a little operation. How was it uncovered?"

Katrina's hands tightened to fists, but her voice remained steady. "The ringleader was dating one of our analysts. He'd managed to steal her security password codes—which is how they gained access in the first place. When she found out, she . . . she turned him in."

"Smart girl. Otherwise she might have been implicated."

Kat shot him a dangerous glare, but he was looking ahead and didn't notice. "She didn't turn him in because she was guilty. She did it because it was the right thing to do."

"Probably," Jack said, missing the underlying anger in her tone. "Still, I'd keep an eye on her, maybe even transfer her to a less critical section. You can't be sure she wasn't in on it."

"I'm sure."

This time it was impossible for Jack to mistake the ice in her voice. He turned to her, astonished by the undiluted fury in her eyes. "Look, I'm sorry. I've seen how much you care about the people who work for you. But you can't be certain—"

"Yes, I can," Kat stated. "I was the analyst."

Hell, thought Jack. *Oh, hell.* "Katrina, believe me. If I'd known—"

"Spare me," Kat said, shaking with anger. "A judge and jury found me innocent, and I'll be damned if I'm going to justify myself to you. I need your help, Jack Fagen, not your sympathy." She spun around and stalked across the lawn, turning back just once to add, "And don't call me Katrina!"

THREE

"She's being difficult," Leonard said.

Katrina hurried along beside him through the computer lab, navigating the imposing maze of cabling and high-tech hardware like a seasoned captain traversing hazardous but familiar waters. Analysts and technicians flitted between the banks of equipment like industrious bees, hectic but content. Katrina usually enjoyed the organized chaos, but today she hardly noticed. She was still fuming over Jack.

"I said, she's being difficult," repeated Leonard.

"Who is?"

"PINK, of course," he answered, obviously annoyed. "What's the matter? You've been preoccupied since you got back from lunch." He lowered his voice, not wanting the other technicians to hear. "It's Fagen, isn't it? I told you it was a mistake to hire him."

"Leonard, I already explained that I didn't have a choice," she said, automatically stepping over one of the bright orange ethernet cables that snaked across the linoleum floor. "So what's up with PINK? She's back, isn't she?"

"Oh, she's back all right. She's just not talking to anyone. She's sulking."

"Maybe she just needs a little understanding," Kat offered. Lord knows, she wasn't the only one.

They arrived at the main console, the nerve center of the entire system. A bank of sophisticated computer equipment and screen monitors stretched halfway across the back wall. The intricate conglomeration would have stumped a mission-control scientist, but Katrina walked directly over to one small screen and sat down. "PINK. PINK, are you there?"

Silence greeted her. Kat frowned with concern and rechecked the sector displays. "This isn't like her. Usually we can't shut her up. Are you sure she's here?"

The analyst sniffed. "She's here. She's just acting like a spoiled brat."

Kat thought Leonard was the one behaving like a spoiled brat. Funny, usually he was the soul of courtesy, sometimes overly so. Apparently Jack's presence had rattled him badly.

He wasn't the only one.

She pulled at the already loose collar of her

blouse and forced herself to concentrate on PINK's computer screen. "She's back, Leonard. That's the important thing. Nobody's perfect. Cut her some slack."

"Glad to hear you say that, Ms. Sheffield," said a deep voice behind her.

Rats, she thought, her shoulders stiffening. Jack Fagen had an absolute talent for catching her at vulnerable moments. She hadn't "cut him any slack" a few minutes ago when she'd walked away from him on the lawn. Now she was advising Leonard to do what she hadn't. She turned around, prepared to defend herself against the knowing smirk she expected to see on his lips. But his smile was soft, not sarcastic, and his eyes held no hint of condemnation. Her anger winked out like a gutted candle flame, leaving a strange stillness behind.

"Let me try," he said, sitting down beside her. "PINK, this is Jack Fagen. I understand you like to gamble. So do I."

A small sound came out of the audio box, but it was drowned out by Leonard saying, "Ms. Sheffield, he shouldn't encourage her bad habits—"

"Leonard, hush," Kat said, more concerned with PINK than with the computer's failings. "It's working. Go on, Jack."

Jack leaned closer to the box, which meant leaning close to Kat. She told herself she didn't like the surge of heat that shot through her system at his nearness, but she didn't draw away.

Jack continued, "I've had a run of bad luck at the track lately. Who do you like in the fourth race?"

The box sputtered to life. "Danny's Girl to show, Ephesians to place, and Rum Runner to win by a nose."

"Glad to have you back, PINK," Katrina said, relieved. Every time PINK left the system she was never quite sure if she would make it back intact. "But what happened to that promise you made me not to leave the system again."

"Forgot," said PINK.

"Forgot? PINK, you've got the combined ROM memory storage of a hundred thousand library books. How could you forget?"

"Woman's prerogative," PINK said. "Jack, want to know who'll win in fifth?"

Jack fought a grin—unsuccessfully. "Later, PINK. Right now I want to talk to you about breaking out of the system. Kat's told me how dangerous it is. She's worried about you. You don't want to worry her, do you?"

"No," PINK admitted. "But must conduct probability studies."

"Who says you can't?" Jack told her. "You tell me the horses, I'll place the bets. We could try it out for a week. Deal?"

"Deal," agreed PINK.

Kat's eyes grew wide in alarm. "Hey, hold on. Humoring PINK is one thing, but placing bets for her is completely out of the question."

Jack placed his hand over PINK's microphone. "Look," he whispered, "you've got a gambling addict here. Tell her to quit cold turkey and you'll be back where you started. Wean her gradually and we may be able to cure her. Besides, this way she's not trying to break out of the system. At least for a week."

A week of not worrying about PINK might not seem like much to Jack, but it was heaven to Katrina. "Good thinking," she acknowledged, giving credit where credit was due. "You think well on your feet."

"Sometimes. And sometimes I step in it royally." He fixed his gaze on her. "I really am sorry for what I said earlier."

Kat stared back into the endless blue of his eyes, feeling lost, and liking it. There should be a law against letting men have eyes like that, especially men as sinfully handsome as Jack Fagen. "It doesn't matter—"

"It does to me," he insisted. "Look, let me make it up to you by taking you to dinner."

Dinner? Alone? With Jack? Now that was a recipe for disaster if she ever heard one. Her body was already having enough trouble remembering they had a *professional* relationship. "Thanks for the offer, but—"

Leonard interrupted her. "Ms. Sheffield, could you come over here and look at this?"

Kat sighed, wondering if Leonard knew how truly terrible his timing was. She told the clearly irritated Jack she'd be right back, then stepped over behind the console to where Leonard was standing. He started speaking before she even opened her mouth.

"I think you should go out with him."

"Leonard, no offense, but my social life is none of your business."

"I'm not talking about your social life," he explained, his long nose twitching. "You could keep an eye on him. Find out what he's up to."

Good old Leonard. The man could read conspiracy into a church picnic. Still, Kat knew he was only trying to help. "Look, I appreciate your concern, but I don't think Jack's up to anything—at least not anything that threatens our system. I know you were against hiring him. I was too. But I think he's going to be a big help to us. Look at how he handled PINK. I respect his knowledge, Leonard. More importantly I trust him."

Her assistant looked at her over the rim of his wire glasses. "That," he told her evenly, "is exactly what you said about Preston Gates."

———◈———————◈———

Katrina Alexandria Sheffield. Age: 28. Occupation: Manager Sheffield Project Development Complex. Marital Status: Single . . .

Jack skimmed the rest of the sheet, noting that once again his superiors had completely missed the point of his request. He'd asked for information that would give him insight into Katrina's character. Instead they'd faxed him a page that read more like a résumé than a psychological profile.

"You're on your own, Jack-boy," he murmured as he stuffed the thin sheet into the inside pocket of his leather jacket. He started the car and pulled into traffic, wishing that his bosses showed half the reliability of this smooth-running machine. Still, reliable or not, he'd agreed to do their dirty work for them. That responsibility didn't end when the job became difficult. Or unsavory.

His mood improved slightly when he pulled up to Katrina's apartment building, an old but elegant structure that dated from Miami's art-deco days. Jack smiled as he looked at the two cement lions that guarded the front door, thinking how unnecessary they were. Katrina's flashpoint temper was all the protection she needed.

He got out of the car and started up the walk, but stopped as Katrina came out to meet him. He stopped breathing too. For the space of several heartbeats he stared at her, wondering if she had any idea what her model figure did to the simple white dress she wore. Or what it did to him.

"Jack," she said pleasantly. "You're right on time."

The small praise sent a surge of pleasure coursing through him. *Careful, Jack,* whispered an inner voice. *You're beginning to care.* Heeding the warning, he turned away, glancing unnecessarily at his watch. "Actually I'm running late," he said, heading back to the car. "We'd better get started if we want to make our dinner reservation."

His terseness caught Katrina by surprise, until she recalled his reputation—coolheaded and cold-hearted, both on and off the job. It was easier this way, she told herself as she slipped into the passenger seat of his black sports coupe. She was having enough trouble not noticing how his midnight-blue polo shirt moved with the muscles of his chest, or how crazy the combined smells of leather and spicy after-shave made her feel. Hot sparks raced along her nerve endings, reminding her of the pure electricity that had consumed her during their skirmish in the garden the night before. She shifted uncomfortably in her seat.

"Is the belt too tight?" asked Jack as he slid into the driver's seat.

"I'm fine," she lied, hoping he wouldn't hear the

catch in her voice. *Better get my mind back on business. Fast.* "I feel I owe you an apology for losing my temper with you."

Jack's mouth curved up in a small smile. "Which time?"

Rich humor laced his voice, pouring through her like warm, dark run. She couldn't resist returning his smile. "The *one* time you didn't deserve it. When you thought I was mixed up in Preston's scheme."

"I never thought . . . Look, it was a stupid thing to say. I have this bad habit of talking first and thinking later."

"You were only thinking about what was best for my system. That's what you were hired to do."

"I shouldn't have jumped to conclusions," Jack stated.

"You were just doing your job," Kat argued.

"I was out of line."

"You were not."

"Was too. It was my fault."

"No, it was *my* fault."

"Argh," Jack said, shaking the steering wheel. "Just once I would like to have a conversation with you that doesn't end in an argument!"

Kat laughed, feeling more lighthearted than she had in an age. She and her cousins used to tumble in and out of arguments all the time. She loved a good sparring match, and wondered why she hadn't had one in such a long time.

As if he'd read her thoughts, Jack said, "You should do that more often."

"What? Argue?"

"Laugh."

Katrina looked down, completely unbalanced. "I laugh," she said defensively.

"Not like that. Not with your whole heart."

A blush burned her cheeks. Damn the man. She was a competent businesswoman, the head of her department. But in Jack's presence she felt like a vulnerable teenager again, tongue-tied and insecure. Like a teenager . . . except that her body ached with a very adult desire. *Hormones*, she thought glumly. *Who needs them?*

Jack took her to a restaurant on the Intercoastal, the waterway that separates Miami Beach from the mainland. Through the picture window Katrina watched cruisers and powerboats glide across the dark water, headed for destinations as far north as Maine. She tried to keep her mind on her purpose for being here, but images of PINK and Leonard faded as she watched the boats slip by. Part of her longed to toss aside her responsibilities and join their adventures.

"You like boats?" asked Jack, noticing her fascination.

"Not the boats, really. It's where they can take me. Going places." She picked up her fork and toyed with a piece of salad. "My mom was Scandinavian, a diplomat's daughter. She had friends and relatives living in just about every country in the world. My dad's idea of a foreign vacation is a deep-sea fishing trip, so Mom and I used to go by ourselves. When I was growing up, I spent almost as much time in Europe and Asia as I did in America."

"Sounds like you inherited some of her wander-lust. Does she still travel?"

Kat's fork stopped. "She died," she said, without looking up.

Inwardly Jack wished hellfire on his information sources. Though he had little affection for his own mother, he could recognize genuine love in others. And genuine grief. "She must have been a wonderful person. And I'm sure her friends still enjoy your visits."

"Who has the time? Between PINK and Einstein I haven't had a moment's rest in a year. E's electronic brain turns to tofu when they announce a sale on the Shopping Channel, and PINK . . . well, I don't dare leave her alone for an instant."

"Einstein's purchases can always be returned," Jack said practically. "And as for PINK . . . why not take her with you? You could set up a clean phone link from any hotel—or casino, come to think of it. I bet she'd love Monte Carlo."

"She'd be deported!"

"Maybe she would," Jack agreed, laughing.

Kat liked his laugh. She liked a lot of things about him—his humor, his intelligence, the way his strong, sensuous fingers curled around the stem of his wineglass. . . . With a start she brought her mind back to the conversation. "I take it you've been to Monte Carlo?"

"Many times," he said, his eyes taking on a soft, distant look. "It always reminds me of a beautiful necklace. The days shine like pearls, the sunsets like warm, red rubies, and the nights . . ." He paused, fixing his blue gaze on her. "The nights burn like the fire in the heart of a diamond. You should go there."

His gaze melted through her, mesmerizing her with his power. She felt the same intense attraction she'd experienced the night before, only worse, because now she wanted the man as well as his body. The rawness of her thoughts shocked her deeply. She picked up her wineglass and steadied her nerves with a sip of the warm, dark liquid. "I would like to go there someday," she said, trying to sound nonchalant. "Not now, though. I've got my work. Besides, it doesn't sound like the sort of place you'd go to alone."

"I wasn't suggesting you go alone."

She set down her glass with a start. *He's kidding*, she thought. But there was no mistaking the blatant desire in his eyes. He was propositioning her. She'd known him a day, and he expected her to go to bed with him. What kind of a woman did he think she was? "You're taking a lot for granted, aren't you?" she said, her temper sparking.

"Am I?"

His words, low and husky, stoked her anger into a different, fiercer heat. Fires, too long banked, burst into flames within her. He was right. Her body ached to be touched, to be held, to be physically loved by someone who knew how to please a woman. She looked at him, confused and a little embarrassed by her reaction.

He sensed her confusion. His gaze softened, and he took her hand in his, curling his strong, surprisingly gentle fingers around her own. "Look, it's simple chemistry. I know you're attracted to me, and I'm incredibly attracted to you. Two consenting adults. Happens every day."

Maybe it happened to him every day. Not to her. He rubbed the tender center of her palm, sending a jolt of lightning through her. She'd never felt this carnal desire for any man before, not even for Preston. "You make it sound so . . . clinical."

His laugh was low and thrillingly sensual. "Believe me, when we make love, it will be anything but clinical."

When. Not "if." Suddenly she remembered who he was—Jack Fagen, a man whose reputation with women was legendary. And, with the exception of Preston, Katrina's experience with men was practically nonexistent. Inexperienced, and coming off a year of celibacy, she was a prime example of what her college classmates used to call a "pushover."

Maybe Jack wasn't trying to deceive her. Maybe he wasn't going to use her love to further his own selfish ends, as Preston had. Maybe . . . but she couldn't take that chance. Slowly, determinedly, she withdrew her hand from his. "I am attracted to you," she admitted, "but I've got . . . responsibilities. To my company, to PINK, and to myself. I can't let my judgment be clouded by emotions. We have a business relationship, Jack. I think it would be better for everyone concerned if we kept it that way."

For a moment his eyes darkened and she thought he was going to argue with her. Part of her wanted him to. But his brow cleared, and he sat back in his seat with a heavy sigh.

"Okay, no Monte Carlo. But I still think you're an incredible woman. If I can't be your lover, at least let me be your friend."

She smiled, surprised at how much she wanted his friendship. Despite her doubts, she admired him:

for his strength, his freedom, and even for his refusal to live by anybody else's rules. Surely she could keep her physical desires in check for the brief time he was here. She lifted her wineglass in a mock salute. "Deal," she agreed, using his familiar expression. "But only if you tell me more stories about your travels."

Jack leaned back in his chair, grinning at her unexpected request. "I'm all yours," he told her.

Kat ignored the double entendre. She twirled her wine, pretending to study the dark, swirling liquid. But more and more it reminded her of the subtle, mesmerizing darkness in Jack's eyes. She set down the glass with a start.

"More wine?"

"No," she stated. *Think of something intelligent to ask. Think of it quick.* "Tell me . . . tell me about your mission in Kuwait, the one Einstein mentioned."

"The top-secret one?"

"Oh." *Well*, she thought bleakly, *he can scratch intelligent off the list.* "I guess you're not supposed to talk about it, are you?"

Technically she was right. He shouldn't tell her about a classified mission, even though any reason for secrecy had long since disappeared. But he wanted to tell her, to bring that eager smile back to her all-too-serious face. He decided to tell the story, and chose not to wonder why it was so easy to break the rules for her.

"Years ago, when I joined the army, they put me into the Mobile Communications Division, mainly because I was a green recruit and too inexperienced to know what a terrible job it was. They sent me to every godforsaken, backwater outpost in the world, with orders to set up state-of-the-art computer communications equipment." He sat back in his chair, smiling wryly at the memory. "It was kind of like digging to China with a soupspoon, but by the time I left the army, I was one of the best in the field.

"Anyway, during the Gulf War the army needed a base of operations set up in Kuwait City. My experience setting up equipment under—well, let's just say less than favorable conditions made me their first choice. They asked, and I said yes. Worst mistake of my life."

"Why?" she asked. "I thought you'd be glad to help out your country."

"The first thing my *country* did," Jack growled, "was pack me and my equipment into a beat-up truck and send me on a bone-jarring ride over the worst back roads in that part of the desert. It was like being a green recruit all over again. They called it camouflage. I call it cruel and unusual punishment."

Kat couldn't suppress a smile at his grim expression. "I'm sure they only did it for your protection."

"You'd have made a great army officer," he commented dryly. "Anyway, we finally made it to the American embassy, the place where I was instructed to set up shop—"

"But the embassy was mined. I saw them defusing the charges after the war on TV."

It felt good, much too good, to have her so concerned about his safety. He'd have to watch that. "The mines weren't as dangerous as they looked," he lied. "Besides, we were very, very careful."

"Were you frightened?"

"Frightened?" he scoffed. He looked at her, prepared to give her the standard answer—that "frightened" and "Jack Fagen" were mutually exclusive terms. But the glib statement died on his tongue. She was wrapped up in the story of his reluctant heroism, amazingly so. Her bright eyes looked at him with an expression dangerously akin to worship. Suddenly he wanted her to see him as a man—not the confident, emotionless hero of his reputation. "Frightened?" he repeated, and added a self-deprecating chuckle. "Katrina, I was scared stiff."

She blinked in surprise at his answer. Then her mouth turned up in a slow, understanding smile. "You don't tell everyone that, do you?"

"Bad for business if I did," he answered, trying to sound nonchalant. Inside, he felt anything but.

Those wide, oh-so-innocent eyes of hers had a way of finding the truth in him like a heat-seeking missile. And telling the truth wasn't the healthiest occupation for a man in his line of work.

He needed to get her mind off him and onto other things. "Maybe I had better get clearance before I tell you the rest of the operation. Meanwhile why don't you tell me a story." He bent toward her and, apparently unconsciously, began to run his finger along the length of her resting arm. "What are your secrets, Katrina?"

She paled, disturbed by the double assault of his question and his touch. Especially his touch. His light, teasing fingers streamed a line of miniature explosions across her skin. Talk about mined! "Secrets? I don't have any secrets."

"No secrets?" His tone admonished. "Not even when you were growing up?"

"Well, sure," she told him. "My cousins and I cornered the market on secrets. There was this one time. . . ."

She launched into a cute, almost sitcomlike story about herself and her relatives, just as he'd hoped she would. He continued to stroke her arm, but now the contact soothed her, subliminally building her trust in him. He listened attentively to her words, mentally filling in the blank areas left by the incomplete fax. He smiled at appropriate intervals, chuckled appropriately, and tried to remember that he wasn't *supposed* to feel like a world-class slime when he was pumping a source for information.

"Lord, watch over me, for the sea is so vast and my boat is so small." Katrina drew back her arm and threw another shell into the night-hushed waves. "Did I say that right?"

"Like you learned it from Sister Barbara herself," Jack said, staring out over the water. "Ha. My shell still went farther."

"You got lucky," she complained. She slipped off her sandals and dug her stockinged toes into the moist sand. Then she flung her shell with all the power and skill she'd used when she consistently won against her cousins. She hadn't expected Jack to challenge her champion standing when she'd told him about her childhood game over dinner. But here they were, on the deserted beach just down the street from her apartment house, tossing pieces of shells into the ocean. She hadn't played this game in years. Now, with the fresh wind in her hair and the salt spray on her cheeks, she wondered why not.

Perhaps because she'd hadn't had someone like Jack to play it with before.

The shell arched above the water, glinting briefly in the bright moonlight before it disappeared beneath the dark, rolling waves.

"Not even close," Jack commented uncharitably.

"Yeah, well I'm out of practice. I almost won."

"Almost won?" Jack sputtered. "Mine was yards ahead of yours. You are such a liar."

"Not like you," she said, crossing her arms decisively in front of her. "There *is* a Sister Barbara, isn't there? Why did you tell me there wasn't?"

Jack looked at the dark sea. He stretched out his arms and breathed in a lungful of the fresh night air. Kat watched his powerful movements and felt a sweet ache in her center. She forced herself to ignore it. They'd agreed to be "just friends," and if ever a man needed a friend, it was Jack.

Moonlight outlined his face, carving his rugged features in pale alabaster. There was something about seeing him silhouetted against the lonely emptiness of the ocean that made her heart go out to him. "Jack?"

He turned back toward her. The faint light glinted off his dark eyes, making them look cold and hard as metal. "You asked why I pretended that Sister Barbara wasn't real. I suppose it was so I could pretend that the other people and things in my past weren't real either. I grew up on the poor side of Chicago. My mom had zero maternal instincts, and the only thing I know about my father is that he disappeared as soon as he found out Mom was pregnant."

Katrina couldn't stand the awful bitterness in his voice, the childhood loneliness that still filled him, even after all these years. "Your mother must have cared about you," she argued. "Why, she paid for you to go to Catholic school, didn't she?"

Jack's smile was as bitter as his voice. "Mom was just religious enough to believe it would count against her in the hereafter if she didn't raise me up in the church. I guess it made up for her getting pregnant out of wedlock. She never missed an opportunity to tell me how I ruined her life. My childhood wasn't exactly 'Leave It to Beaver' material."

Katrina tried valiantly to smile. "Whose is?"

"Yours." He turned up the beach, walking back toward her apartment. "It's getting late. I'd better go."

Kat fell in step beside him. "Listen, Jack Fagen. Don't go thinking my life was so perfect, because it wasn't. I had my share of troubles. I . . . I was the tallest kid in school, counting boys. I didn't have a date until I was seventeen, and that was with a guy who kissed like a potato."

Jack stopped. "A potato?"

"Yeah, well, that's how I remember it. Anyway, the point is that nobody's life is perfect. And it's those nonperfect parts that help make us wiser and more understanding. 'That which does not kill us makes us stronger.'"

Jack's eyes lost their metallic glint, and his mouth curved into a slow smile. "You are the only person I know who can draw ancient wisdom out of a 'potato kisser.' Unbelievable. I'm glad we're friends."

Normally Katrina would have thought so, too, but at the moment she didn't feel much like a friend. Standing so close to him, with the hush of the waves behind them and the shimmering moon above, was almost more than her senses could bear. She wanted so much more from him than friendship, and the violence of her desire made her shudder.

Jack saw the shudder, and misread it. "Here," he said, taking off his leather jacket and slipping it around her shoulders. "This will warm you up."

He didn't know the half of it. His heat, his smell permeated the jacket, sending her temperature sky-rocketing. Cold she was not. Feeling guilty, she tried to take it off. "I really don't need this."

Jack put his hands on her shoulders and looked her in the eye. "You'll keep it on. That's an ord . . ." The words died on his tongue.

Suddenly things changed. His hands tightened possessively on her shoulders, and his eyes grew dark and wide. She knew he was going to kiss her. She also knew she wasn't going to stop him. Leonard might call her a traitor. Hell, maybe she *was* a traitor. But she couldn't help it. She wanted Jack's kiss more than she'd wanted anything in her life. She closed her eyes and parted her lips.

His hands dropped away. Startled, she opened her eyes and saw him turning away. "Like I said, it's late. You can give the jacket back to me in the morning."

She hurried after him. The Terminator was back, that cold shell that hid his every emotion. Or hid the emotions he didn't have. The switch was so abrupt that suddenly Kat wasn't sure of anything anymore. Except that it hurt. Had his friendship for her been a game, an act to gain her confidence? My God, had she fallen for the same line all over again?

Now she really was cold. She pulled the jacket around her and heard the unexpected crackle of paper. She patted the jacket pockets and pulled a crumpled fax sheet from the inside pocket. "Jack," she said as she started to unfold it, "I found this in the pocket. Do you want—"

She got no further. Jack's mouth covered hers in a sudden, shattering kiss. Shocked, Kat stood absolutely still, powerless to do anything but let his moist, impossibly sensual lips explore her own.

This is insane, she thought, but sanity ceased to be an option as his kiss deepened. White fire shot through her veins, thickening her blood to slow, burning honey. The fax fell to the ground, unheeded. She reached up and tangled her hands in his thick hair. Her mouth opened under his, allowing his invasion, welcoming it.

He dropped his hands to her waist, pulling her against his hard, scorching body. The heat of his arousal branded her, and she groaned her primitive pleasure into his mouth. Instinct consumed her. She wanted him in her, buried in her aching center, taking her as strong men have claimed their women since time began. She'd never felt such wild, primal hunger for a man, not even with Preston—

Preston! Sanity returned in a rush. She pulled out of Jack's arms and stared at him, horrified by her actions. She couldn't believe it. This man had just walked away from her, playing with her emotions as deftly as Preston ever had, and she was a pair of stockings away from making hedonistic love to him on the beach. How did she know he didn't have some secret agenda of his own?

Appalled, she realized that a moment ago she wouldn't have cared if he did.

Jack reached out for her. "I'm sorry. I didn't mean—"

She backed away, shaking her head. "That's the point. I don't know what you mean, or even who you are. Leonard thinks you're up to something. Are you?"

Jack raked his fingers through his hair. "Believe me, Katrina, I'd never do anything to hurt you."

"Funny, but that's exactly what Preston said. Just do right by my system, Jack, or I'll make you wish you were never born." She turned and headed down the block to her apartment building. "And quit calling me Katrina!"

He called after her, but she didn't turn back. He stood motionless for several minutes, his shoulders bowed down as if carrying an unseen weight. Finally he bent down and picked up the crumpled fax sheet that Katrina had dropped while they were kissing. Then he savagely ripped it into tiny, indistinguishable pieces.

FOUR

"Just one more."

Jack continued to study the jumble of complex schematic diagrams spread haphazardly across his desk. "No, PINK," he said firmly. "It's late and I've got too much work to do."

"Please," PINK said, her electronic voice full of anguish. "Last time. Promise."

Jack's hard-set mouth turned into a reluctant smile. During the past week he'd learned that PINK's promises had about as much lasting value as junk bonds, but he found the con-artist computer hard to resist all the same. He set down his drafting pencil and raised his hand to rub his tired eyes. Then he turned to the small speaker sitting on the corner of his office desk. "Okay. Give me the stats."

"Crazy Legs to place in third race at Arlington.

Probability of success eighty-nine percent. A sure thing."

Jack's smile became an outright grin. "That so?" he said as he jotted the statistics on a nearby notepad. "Well, you certainly don't lack confidence. Still, you could use a lesson or two in restraint."

"Learn restraint. Piece of toast," she commented brightly, and signed off.

Jack gave a short, humorless laugh. Up to a week ago he would have agreed with her. He'd always prided himself on his cool head, his ability to make crucial decisions under fire, unclouded by emotions. But that ability had evaporated the moment he'd kissed Katrina.

It was supposed to be a simple distraction, calculated to divert her attention from the incriminating fax. But all calculations, simple or otherwise, vanished when his lips covered hers. *Calculation?* he thought wryly. *Try cataclysmic!*

Lightning had arced between them, burning through him like liquid fire. Her mouth met his with an eagerness he'd never experienced with any other women—wanton, yet ripe with sweet, totally captivating innocence. Passion was nothing new to him, but this thing they'd shared was something more, something as essential to him as the food he ate or the air he breathed. That single kiss had ripped away all his carefully constructed emotional defenses, and the crazy thing was, he wanted nothing more than to kiss her again.

Slim chance of that, Jack-boy. He picked up the drafting pencil and tossed it down again in frustration. Katrina had done her level best to avoid him this past week, and when she did meet him, it was in the company of Leonard or one of her other analysts. It didn't take a rocket scientist to figure out why. She'd trusted him, and like a cad he'd taken advantage of that trust. She'd asked him point-blank if he was being straight with her, her beautiful eyes bright with pain and distrust and a crazy kind of hope. It was the hope that tore him apart. He'd wanted to hold her against him, to smooth her hair and tell her that everything would be all right. But that, of course, would have been yet another lie.

Frustrated thoughts spun 'round and 'round in his mind, making it impossible to concentrate on his work. Sighing, he looked at his watch. Eleven-thirty. He might as well go home and get some sleep. *Or try to*, he thought grimly. Lately guilt over his situation with Katrina had kept him awake at night—guilt, coupled with the most erotic dreams he'd experienced since puberty.

"Just one more."

"PINK—" he began, but stopped before he lost his temper. After all it wasn't PINK's fault that he was in a foul mood. "Look, I'm dog tired. I'll place your bet in the morning."

"Too late then," PINK moaned. "Bet for Australian races. Be over by morning. I'll ask Kat to do it."

"You will not," he said sternly. "PINK, don't you dare call Kat and wake her up to—"

"Don't have to. She's here."

Jack's sleepy eyes snapped open. "Katrina's here? You mean, here in the building?"

"She's in lab," explained the computer. "Moving cabinet. Now, about my bet . . ."

But Jack was no longer listening. He'd already gotten up from his desk and left his office, striding down the hallway toward the computer lab. Alone, without anyone to run interference for her, Katrina would have no choice but to listen to him. And he'd make her listen to him, even if he had to tie her down with ethernet cables to do it.

Katrina didn't like the computer room at night. The lab, so noisy and bustling during the day, quieted to an eerie, empty silence after hours. High-tech equipment clicked and whirred with clockwork precision, but the mechanical efficiency was depressingly hollow, like a smile without warmth, or a body without a soul. Kat had been struggling for fifteen minutes to push the massive CPU cabinet back against the wall. In the unsettling silence, every minute stretched out like a year.

"Want some help?"

Kat looked up, startled by the unexpected voice, and saw Jack charging across the lab to her rescue. The sight of a friendly face in the coldly impersonal room filled her with welcome warmth, until she remembered that Jack Fagen had more in common with a dragon than with a rescuing white knight. "I can handle it," she said, squaring her pained shoulders despite the discomfort.

"I never said you couldn't," Jack said, his mouth pulling into a smile. "I just asked if you wanted some help. Do you?"

Katrina glanced between Jack and the big cabinet, weighing her options. Stubborn pride vied with the reality of aching shoulder blades. Reality won. She moved from the center to the right front side of the CPU cabinet and nodded toward the empty left side. "Be my guest."

Jack and Kat leaned their shoulders against the cold metal siding. Together they pushed, pulled, and shoved the heavy cabinet back against the wall. When they were done, Jack stepped back and kneaded his upper arm. "Good grief. What's that thing made of? Lead?"

"I think so. It's shielded."

"Oh, swell," he said, working his strained muscles. "Mind giving me a little warning next time I offer to play knight-errant?"

Kat challenged him with a grin. "So you're only into situational chivalry?"

"Beats sciatica." His expression remained grim, but there was a definite gleam of humor in his eyes. "Lord, I can't remember the last time my arm was this sore. Probably not since I went after Quicksilver."

"Quicksilver?" Kat said, her curiosity sparked.

"That was his code name. He was a Soviet operative working out of different locations in North America. You know, back when Russians were the bad guys."

"He was a spy?"

"Not exactly. More like an independent hacker. He slipped in and out of government computer systems like . . . well, like the liquid metal he was named for. But he never stayed in more than five minutes and I couldn't get a fix on him."

Kat could imagine. Five minutes isn't much time to pinpoint a precise location on a continent, especially when that location keeps moving. "How did you catch him?"

"I bamboozled the sucker," Jack said, justifiably proud of his accomplishment. "I set up a dummy file of government 'secrets.' Lots of official-sounding double-talk, but no content. I think the most classi-fied piece of information in there was the price of roast beef in the officers' mess. But the file was big and it took a full hour to download. Quicksilver snapped up the bait, and—"

"You reeled him in," Kat finished, caught up in Jack's ingenuity. "Who was he?"

"Now, that's the funny part. The elusive, infa-mous Quicksilver turned out to be a third-rate coun-try singer who traveled around the country in a beat-to-death Chevy van. After his gigs he would set up his laptop, sell a government secret or two, and deposit his earnings into a tidy Cayman Island–bank nest egg." Jack flexed his fingers, apparently making sure that they still worked. "He was a lousy singer, but a first-class hacker."

"But what does Quicksilver have to do with your arm?"

"It wasn't Quicksilver so much as Quicksilver's guitar," he answered, finally losing his battle with his grin. "Along with being a first-class hacker, he had a first-class swing."

Katrina laughed, enjoying the humorous story. Enjoying Jack. Too late she realized her mistake. Shared smiles made her let down her guard with Jack, made her remember how much she honestly liked the man. And opened the door to the mael-strom of emotions she'd struggled all this week to control. The ache in her shoulders was nothing compared with the ache in her heart. She looked away, and took a quick, perfunctory glance at her watch. "Thanks for your help, but it's late and we ought to be—"

"Kat, don't."

"Don't what?" she asked, striving for brightness.

"Don't run away from me again."

The pain in his voice drew her back to him. She saw the tense expectancy in the set of his jaw, the hint of shadows under his eyes. But the look in his eyes was anything but tired. Heat radiated through her body, unnerving her completely. This situation was getting out of hand. She had to end it. Now. "Jack, rehashing what happened isn't going to do either of us any good. We agreed to keep our relationship professional—"

"That was before."

"Before what?"

He leaned closer, so close she could feel his hot breath stroking her cheek. "You tell me. I see those circles under your eyes. PINK would give me ten to one that you haven't been getting much sleep this past week."

Kat gasped, remembering the midnight hours when she'd allowed herself to indulge in the forbidden fantasy of having Jack in bed beside her. Potent, spectacularly indecent images flooded her mind, making her blush to the roots of her hair. "I've . . . I've had a lot on my mind lately," she hedged.

"Me too," he said huskily. "Like your lips, your hair, your impossibly long legs." He lifted his hand and gently traced her cheekbone with his finger. "Why are you avoiding me? What are you so afraid of?"

"You wouldn't understand."

"Try me," he said, his words edged with desperation. "Hell, Katrina, you're not the only one lying awake nights."

His masculinity was overwhelming, but even more devastating was his admission of need for her. The thought of him wanting her the same way she wanted him burned through her like a stiff shot of hard, rough moonshine. She longed to slip into his arms and make those nighttime fantasies a reality, but her mind fought for control. She couldn't allow herself to give in to sexual need and damn the consequences. Not again. "Please," she said hoarsely. "Don't call me Katrina. Preston used to call me that."

"Preston!" Jack said, his tone making the name a curse. He dropped his hand to his side and balled it into a tight fist. "What is it with you and this guy? Look, I'm not Preston. This past week I've been busting my hump just to prove to you how un-Preston-like I am."

"I know you've been working hard and I appreciate—"

"I don't want your *appreciation*," Jack said, his eyes glittering dangerously. "What I want is for you to talk to me. Is that so much to ask?"

It's the world, thought Kat, but she was going to do it anyway. Her need to make him understand was greater than her need to hide from the pain. She stepped away from him and looked down so she wouldn't have to see his face while she told him her story. She could stand seeing anger in his eyes, but not pity.

"I told you Preston's lawyer tried to prove I was involved in the embezzlement scam. What I didn't tell you is *how* he tried to prove it. He brought up every aspect of our relationship in open court, even"—she paused, taking a steadying breath— "even the most personal, private ones."

Jack breathed a low curse, but Katrina didn't seem to hear him. She hugged her arms to her body and continued speaking. "You've got to give the devil his due. Preston's lawyer was extremely thorough. He talked about what we did, how we did it, even how many times I reached . . . I was in love with Preston, but his lawyer made my love sound cheap, even pathetic. He made me out to be some spineless, love-starved female who'd do anything for . . . well, I think you get the picture."

Jack got the picture, all right. He thought he'd gotten used to injustice—Lord knows, he'd seen enough of it—but hearing what Preston had done to her made him angrier than anything had in a long time. "Katrina, I'm so—"

"Don't say it," Kat said, spinning to face him. "For heaven's sake, don't say you're sorry for me. I did what I had to do."

"Kat—"

Katrina ignored him, knowing that if she didn't get the words out now, she never would. "Preston offered me a deal: My silence for his. 'Eat hot death,' I told him. I walked into that courtroom and told the unvarnished truth, no matter how much it hurt. It was my testimony that put him away, my words—"

"Kat, be quiet!"

Katrina did, startled to silence by the authority in his voice. He looked down at her, his arms crossed imposingly across his expansive chest, his face stern and slightly annoyed. There wasn't an ounce of patronizing pity in him. "If you would let me get a word in," he stated quietly, "you would know that I wasn't going to say I was sorry for you. I was going to say I was proud of you."

She blinked in surprise. "Proud?"

His eyes softened, and the corner of his stern mouth twitched up in a smile. "You didn't run away. It doesn't matter what Preston said about you—

anyone who's seen those flashing violet eyes of yours would know what he said was a crock. What does matter is that you didn't run away from your problems. You dealt with Preston. Then you came back to this system and made it work."

Kat shook her head. She didn't deserve that kind of respect, not by a long shot. "I didn't have a choice," she explained as she self-consciously fingered the sleeve of her blouse. "I couldn't desert PINK, and Leonard, and the other technicians. Anyone would have done the same."

"Not in my experience." Jack unfolded his arms and took her shoulders, turning her to face him. His warm, confident grasp sent shivers of pleasure down her arms. Then he reached up and gently tilted her chin so she had no choice but to look directly into his fiercely blue eyes. "Listen to me. Most people would have taken the easy way out, and kept their mouths shut. But not you. I've never met anyone like you, Ms. Katrina Alexandria Sheffield."

The frank admiration in his gaze turned her knees to water. "I've never met anyone like you, Jack Fagen," she said unsteadily.

"Good," he said. Then he kissed her.

He kissed her gently, with a sweet tenderness that cherished her more than words ever could. Nestled in his arms, she felt fragile as a delicate blossom, an unusual comparison for a woman who could wrestle most of the men she knew to the ground. His lips moved across her face, placing moist, almost reverent kisses on her cheeks, her nose, and her closed eyelids. It was not the kind of kiss she'd expected to receive from the emotionless Jack Fagen, and it devastated her twice as much as the passionate caresses they'd shared last week.

He took his time, and when he was through, he pulled her to him, holding her against the wonderful comfort of his hard-packed chest. She felt the steady rhythm of his muscles as they rose and fell with his breathing, and heard his strong heart beating close to her own. Katrina had a vague suspicion that she shouldn't be letting Jack hold her like this, but she couldn't exactly remember why. All thoughts were lost in the warm peace that filled her as she snuggled deeper into the warm security of Jack's embrace.

He stroked her hair, laughing softly. "For a hellcat you've got a lot of kitten in you. That's what I think I'll call you. Kitten."

She lifted her head and smiled sweetly. "You do and I'll break your jaw."

"Ha. You would too," he said, accenting his words with a low, sexy chuckle. "Remind me never to get on the wrong side of you in a fight. Between major computer installations, wandering computers, and sleazy defense lawyers, I doubt there's anything you can't handle."

"Maybe," she said, suddenly serious. "I think I could handle anything, as long . . . as long as you were being straight with me."

She'd startled him. She could see it in his eyes, and feel it in the sudden tensing of his body. His expression hardened and she sensed him retreating behind the wall of icy reserve that had earned him his emotionless reputation. She was losing him. Part of her wanted to cry out, to take back her words, and to believe in him completely, whether he spoke the truth or not. Her heart almost broke at the loss.

Suddenly the change stopped. His eyes lost their hooded expression, and their former warmth returned like dawn to a morning sky. He reached up and softly brushed something from the edge of her cheek. Only then did she realize she was crying.

"To hell with this," he growled, his mouth hardening into a firm, resolute line. "Katrina, I—"

He got no further. Suddenly the room was filled with enough noise to wake the dead. Alarm sirens.

"The system!" Kat cried, pulling out of his embrace. "Someone's breaking into the system!"

Panicking, she ran across the computer room, hearing Jack's footfalls pounding a step behind her. Together they rushed to the command console and scanned the various monitor screens for the problem. Jack was the first to spot it. "There," he said, pointing to one of the top-level monitors. "It's in

PINK's sector. She must have brought a piggyback virus into the system."

"But PINK hasn't been out for days," Kat argued.

"She didn't need to," he said, quickly seating himself at the main keyboard. "These things can be set like time bombs to go off days, even weeks after the fact." He looked at his watch, noting that the second hand was barely thirty seconds past twelve. "Midnight sharp. We're dealing with a pro."

Kat paled. Her worst fears were coming true, but she was determined not to lose her head. She looked at the overhead monitor, watching the pattern of the disturbance, trying to determine its character. "It looks like it's replicating itself, replacing pieces of PINK with pieces of itself."

"That makes sense," he said, typing furiously. "It's probably sending her down the lines in byte-sized chunks. If we don't stop it soon, there'll be nothing left of her."

"Nothing," Kat repeated. She looked at the spreading virus, feeling helpless. She was totally out of her depth. "We've got to save her, Jack. We've got to."

Jack flashed her his trademark grin. "We will. *Nobody* messes with Jack Fagen."

Katrina looked at him, loving his cocky self-assurance, his absolute belief in his own excellence.

A warning voice told her that she was out of her depth here, too, but she didn't have time to dwell on it. "Okay. What can I do to help?"

He glanced at the monitor. "Cut back the power. Electricity's like oxygen to a virus. Cut the power and we cut its growth."

"Right," she said, stepping to the circuit box. She flipped off most of the power circuits and turned the main dial down to quarter power. She looked back at the overhead monitor. The virus's growth had slowed considerably.

"Jack, it's working!"

Fagen didn't share her enthusiasm. "But it's still growing," he said, frowning. "I've started up my security subsystems to plug the hole, but they need time. Can you cut the power down more?"

Katrina made a quick scan of the power grid. "I don't dare. Any lower and we'll lose the security net. The system would be left wide open. PINK wouldn't have a chance."

"She hasn't got much of one now," he admitted. Leaning back, he raked his hands through his hair, clearly frustrated. "Think, Fagen. Cutting power won't do it. Think of another way."

Katrina knew she should be watching the monitor, but she found it impossible to look away from Jack. Cool courage showed in every line on his profile, an absolute refusal to give up under any circumstances. She knew he was fighting with all he had to save her PINK, and not just because it was his job. He cared. He might be a self-centered opportunist, but he was straight-arrow honest when it came to his work. If only that honesty carried over into his personal relationships. Into his kisses . . .

"I've got it!" Jack said, turning to her. "Turn up the power."

"What? You just told me to turn it down."

"I haven't time to explain," he said, riveting her with his startling blue eyes. "Trust me, Kitten. This is what I do best."

She nodded, hoping it was her good sense that made her trust him and not the crazy joy she felt when he used that ridiculous nickname. Sometimes it was damned inconvenient to be a woman. She stepped to the circuit box and turned up the power full, sending a surge of electricity through the system. Suddenly she realized what Jack was trying to do. "A power surge," she said. "Of course!"

She'd just gotten out the last word when the power hit maximum and the surge-protector system took over. The lights faded and the monitor screens went blank as the system automatically broke its power connections and shut down all outside transmissions. Every computer system had a fail-safe power-surge backup system to protect the computer from lightning strikes and other electrical malfunctions. Katrina held her breath, hoping that the connection to the virus source had been severed in time.

One by one the systems automatically switched back on, and the monitor screens jumped to life. Katrina looked at Jack and saw uncertainty in his eyes. Now that the crisis was over, his bravado had left him, like the wind going out of a sail. She reached out and grasped his hand, giving it a heartfelt squeeze. Personal feelings aside, they were partners. They were in this thing together.

Cautiously she spoke. "Einstein, are you here?"

The speaker by the console bank crackled to life. "Boy, have I got a headache."

Jack gave her a guarded grin. "Circuit overload. It'll pass."

Katrina nodded. She took a deep breath. "PINK?"

For a long, heart-stopping moment there was only silence. Katrina clasped Jack's hand, feeling his power flow into her, strengthening her. She asked again, more clearly this time. "Stop kidding around, PINK. Answer me."

The speaker hissed to life. "Way cool! Better than horse racing."

"PINK!" Kat cried. She dropped Jack's hand and ran to the speaker, circling it with her arms. It was a foolish gesture, but she didn't care. "PINK, you're okay."

"Ready for trifecta," PINK assured her.

Katrina looked up and met Jack's eyes. Nothing had changed between them—she still didn't know if she could trust him, and she was confused as hell by her feelings, but for the moment it didn't matter. She looked at him, her whole heart in her eyes. "Thanks," she said. She started to say more, but at that moment the main door to the computer room burst open. People poured in—security guards, night-shift programmers, even cleaning people who'd heard the alarm. Everyone had heard the sirens and wanted to know what had happened.

Katrina gave them a quick summary of the events, and soon everyone was slapping Jack on the back, congratulating him on a job well done. Jack barely heard their praises. He was thinking of the final piece of information he'd seen on the computer screen, the screen he'd deleted the moment people began to enter the computer room. Even Katrina hadn't seen it.

The information consisted of the encrypted system code, the personal log-on identifier used by the saboteur/hacker. Like most codes it followed a pattern, and Jack's experience enabled him to determine not only where the code had been entered, but who had entered it.

Jack looked at Katrina and her surrounding crowd of well-wishers, a grim suspicion beginning to form in his mind. The code had been entered from inside the building, indicating that the hacker was a Sheffield employee. The rest of the encryption named that employee, and the log-on evidence pointed directly and irrefutably to . . . Katrina.

FIVE

The next morning Katrina took a good look at herself in the bathroom mirror. Her hair was a mess and her eyes were still blurred with sleep, but it didn't matter. For the first time since the humiliating trial, she felt she liked the woman she saw staring back at her. A heaviness she hadn't even been aware of lifted from her shoulders. She glanced outside at the white gulls skimming lightly over the water, thinking she felt a little like flying herself.

With a touch of her old spirit, she ignored the conservative taupe suit she'd laid out and headed into the depths of her walk-in closet. In the back she found a floral-print dress she hadn't worn in over a year. The snug bodice molded to her trim figure like a glove, while the skirt flowed softly around her hips and long legs. She slipped on a pair of white sandals and finished the outfit with the ivory rose-cut earrings that had once belonged to her mother. She looked in the mirror at the finished product, feeling elegant and feminine, and just a little bit sexy.

She wondered, shyly, if a certain other person would think she looked sexy too.

Her confidence rose a notch when her new look provoked wolf whistles from the construction site next to her office building. The security guard at the front door did a double take when he saw her, and the receptionist gave her the thumbs-up sign as she passed. She felt as if someone had filled her with pure sunshine. The gulls, she decided, had nothing on her.

Jack was responsible for her newfound assurance. His acceptance of her had helped her to accept herself. Things had gone from crazy to chaos last night, and she'd never gotten the chance to thank him for what he'd done for PINK. Or for what he'd done for her.

She walked down the hallway to his office, eager to thank him for all he'd done. But as his office got closer her confidence wavered. Maybe last night had meant more to her than it had meant to him. He was a man of the world, and she was a too-tall woman who had a bad habit of reading too much into a kiss. Once nicknamed "beanpole" by her teenage peers, she'd had little experience with men, sophisticated or otherwise. A kiss might not mean more than a handshake to a worldly man like Jack. Oh, God, she thought as she reached his office door, what if he was only taking pity on her?

She had almost decided to turn around when she noticed that his office door was slightly ajar. Through the crack she could see him sitting at his desk, his bearded chin propped on his hands as he stared into nothingness. Her heart made a strange, sideways thump in her chest as she studied his rough-hewn features and thought about the lonely little boy he'd once been. His kisses might not mean anything, but his need for a friend was all too real. He'd asked her to be that friend. She reached up and gave the door frame a hesitant knock.

He didn't answer. He was wrapped in thought, his expression as coldly remote as a granite cliff. For a moment she considered leaving and coming back another time, but something deep inside told her he needed her. She knocked louder. "Jack, it's Kat—Katrina. Can I come in?"

This time he heard her. He looked up, and met her gaze with a cool, oddly emotionless glance. He nodded to the chair in front of his desk, his grim expression unchanged. "Come in, Kat."

Kat. Not Kitten. Not even Katrina. There was no warmth in his tone, and no warmth in his manner. She sat down, perplexed by his coolness. "Are you feeling all right?"

All right? he thought. He was dying inside. Being in the same room with her raised his temperature twenty degrees. He'd spent most of the morning steeling himself for this moment, but nothing could have prepared him for the hammer blow that hit him when he looked into her beguiling, innocent eyes.

In her bright floral dress she looked like all spring gardens rolled into one. Her shining hair held the color of sunshine, but stirred something like hellfire in the pit of his abdomen. Her eyes held all the sweet surrender he'd longed to see in them last night, and his arms ached to hold her. It wouldn't have taken much to reach out and pull her close to him. Not much, just trust. And trusting her was the one thing he couldn't afford to do, not after that damning encryption he'd seen in the computer file. "I'm fine, Kat. Now, is there something I can do for you? Or . . . is there something you want to tell me?"

"Well, yes, there is," Katrina said, amazed at his perception. "I wanted to thank you for what you did last night."

Jack's mouth hardened into a grim line. If Kat hadn't known better, she would have sworn he was disappointed by her expression of gratitude. Confused, she continued. "I didn't get a chance to tell you how much I appreciated what you did for me."

Jack waved her praise aside and said coolly, "It's

my job to maintain your system's integrity. No need to thank me for doing my job."

"I wasn't talking about my system. I was talking about me."

Jack said nothing, but Katrina thought she saw a small, almost imperceptible softening around the corners of his mouth. At least she hoped she saw it. She hurried on, regretting that she'd been born without the subtlety that every other woman on earth seemed to possess. "Since the trial I've felt empty inside, like I've been going through the motions of life without really living it. I lost my faith in people. Worse, I lost my faith in myself. But last night you gave me back some of that faith. You believed in me and . . . oh, hell, you probably think I sound like an idiot."

An idiot was the last thing he thought she sounded like. He stared at her, entranced by the play of emotions on her exquisite, heartbreakingly open face. The rose staining her delicate cheeks was too real to be counterfeit, and her eyes met his without a trace of guile, undermining his cool steel defenses. Lord, he'd rather face down a pack of third-world revolutionaries than those impossibly lovely eyes.

Kat lifted her chin defiantly. "I wish you'd say something," she said, smiling uncertainly.

The smile decided him, that and her determined but slightly quivering chin. Jack's profession had trained him to doubt everyone's motives, but he'd lived by his wits too long not to trust his instincts. And his instincts told him that Katrina was not a criminal. She was a beautiful, vulnerable woman who'd been horribly hurt by a man she'd trusted. He damn well wasn't going to add to her pain. "Katrina—"

The phone rang, shattering the moment. Jack reached out and snatched up the receiver before the second ring. "What is it?" he barked.

"It's Leonard. I'm trying to find Ms. Sheffield. Would you by chance know where—"

"She's here, but she's busy," Jack said curtly. Honestly, Leonard did have the poorest timing. "She's busy right now. I'll have her call you back."

"Oh, please, I really must speak with her now. I'm afraid there's a problem in the computer lab."

By Jack's count there was a problem in the computer lab every five minutes, which was strange considering how well the system was constructed. And those problems almost always landed squarely on Katrina's shoulders . . . shoulders that already carried more than their fair share of responsibility.

Well, for once Jack was going to see that she got a breather. "Look, Heep, can't you handle—"

Katrina heard him mention her associate's name. Instantly she put aside her own concerns. "Is that Leonard?"

Jack covered the receiver with his hand. "Yeah. He says there's a problem, but—"

"I'd better take it. I'm sure Leonard wouldn't have called if it wasn't important."

Jack doubted it, but he had little choice. He knew how much the system meant to her. He handed Kat the phone and watched her listen to Leonard's explanation. He could almost see her shoulders droop under the weight of this additional burden.

His mouth pulled into a grim line. How long would it be before her selfless devotion to her system crushed the life right out of her?

Eventually she sighed, and handed the receiver back to him. "One of the programmers made a nasty remark about PINK in front of Einstein. E called the programmer a 'waste of good protoplasm' and now both of them are refusing to work together. I'd better get down there and straighten things out." She stood up and smoothed out the already smooth material of her dress. "Anyway, I'm glad I got the chance to talk with you." *Even if I did make a complete fool of myself.*

"Katrina?"

He'd used her full name. She paused at his office door, afraid to hope that it meant anything. "Yes?"

Jack cleared his throat. "Look, when I've found out who—I mean, when I've finished restructuring your security system . . ." *What then?* he wondered. What could he offer her? Not promises. Certainly not the truth. She deserved so much more than his orders allowed him to give. He opened his mouth, searching for something. "When I've finished, maybe we could try another game of shell toss."

She looked at him, her eyes wide and puzzled. Then she smiled with a trace of her usual moxie. "If you don't mind losing," she said, and slipped out of his office.

Jack rested his elbows on his desk and propped his head on his fists, staring at the empty place she'd left behind. For a long moment he sat still as stone, then he broadly swept aside the jumble of schematics. He reached in his top drawer and pulled out a legal pad and a pen, and began a concise and detailed list of all the steps he'd have to take to prove Katrina innocent of last night's sabotage. It would mean more work and more hours, not to mention some highly questionable system manipulation, but that hardly mattered. He was going to prove she had nothing to do with PINK's virus—even if he had to work around the clock to do it.

A week later Jenny walked into Katrina's office unannounced, and what she saw brought a smile to her face.

"It's very pretty, Ms. Sheffield."

Kat, startled by her secretary's unexpected appearance, hastily stuffed the garment she'd been holding up to herself back into her briefcase. "I was just . . ."

Jenny's smile broadened at her boss's embarrassment. "You were just looking at a racy red silk teddy. It'll look spectacular on you. I'm sure he'll think so, too."

Kat turned almost as crimson as the hidden teddy. "I don't know what you mean."

Jenny grinned. "Oh, come on. I'd have to be blind not to notice the looks you and Mr. Fagen have been giving each other this past week. Talk about hot! Nuclear reactors could take lessons—"

"Jenny, don't you have some filing to do or something?" Kat interrupted. "And don't you have to do it somewhere else?"

Jenny laughed good-naturedly. "Actually I was about to leave for the day. I just came in to give you this," she said, handing Katrina a small, padded package, "and to tell you that Leonard is on his way up to see you. He said he has some important printouts for you to look at."

"Well, if Leonard says they're important, I'm sure they are," Kat said, though she wished her associate hadn't waited until the end of the day to talk with her. She was exhausted. Ever since the PINK episode, the whole computer department had been on edge. System security had been breached, and no one could be a hundred percent certain it wouldn't happen again. Tempers flared. Trivial incidents sparked titanic arguments, and she'd spent most of her time soothing her programmers' ruffled feathers.

Which was funny, considering what a sorry state her own "feathers" were in. "Just leave the door open on your way out, Jenny."

"Will do," the younger woman said, heading out. But she stopped at the door and looked back. "I meant what I said about that teddy. You'll knock his socks off. Among other things . . ."

"Out," Katrina said, shooing her away. Deep down she appreciated Jenny's encouragement, but the kindly-meant words brought on a host of insecurities. True, Jack's heated gazes could make her insides sizzle like butter on a skillet, but they were few and far between. Most of the time he was so focused on his job, he hardly noticed her. Sometimes she wondered if he truly cared about her at all.

Trouble was, she cared about him. A lot. She'd noticed the hollows under his eyes, the dog-tired weariness that even his iron control couldn't suppress. Worried, she'd suggested that he take a day off, and even hinted that she might be willing to join him. He'd gruffly declined, brushing off both her and her offer like he'd brush off an irritating gnat. She hadn't realized she could feel so hurt.

She started to open the package that Jenny had delivered, but her mind kept drifting back to Jack. His feelings for her might have ended, but hers for him were still clicking along at a frantic rate. He left her hot, bothered, and confused, with an embarrassing desire to buy ridiculously inappropriate lingerie. *Dummy*, she chided herself. *Women are supposed to buy racy teddies when they've got a guy, not when they don't*.

Irritated at her folly, she pulled apart the package and dumped the contents out on her desk. She'd expected the package to contain a transistor or a computer chip. Instead it yielded a gold chain necklace, exquisitely wrought. Hanging from the center of the delicate chain was a single, polished shell. Even before she looked at the card, she knew it had come from Jack.

Deal, it read.

Enchanted, she lifted the chain and slipped it over her head. The shell fell lightly against her blouse, settling directly above her heart. She knew the gift was a promise, a way of telling her he still cared about her, despite his gruff actions. She reached up and clasped her hand around the bright, precious shell.

A shadow fell across her desk. "Ms. Sheffield, I'm sorry to disturb you."

"That's all right, Leonard," Kat said, dropping the shell. "What did you want to see me about?" *And please, make it quick*, she added silently.

Leonard sighed reluctantly. "I warned you—I did warn you—that Mr. Fagen was up to something."

Katrina remembered the conversation they'd had on Jack's first day—a lifetime ago. She smiled indulgently. "Believe me, Leonard. Jack's the last person you should suspect. He's just about the most honest, most dependable—"

The analyst interrupted her. "But this time I have proof." He dumped a thick computer printout on Katrina's desk. "Look at the highlighted parts."

Kat dutifully flipped back a few pages. It was a hard-copy printout of the system log, the account of all the hundreds of transactions that took place within her system. Leonard had highlighted a couple of transactions on each page. At first she couldn't see a pattern, then she realized that all the transactions were accessing her files. Jack's transactions. Jack was tracking her movements through the system. "But why?" she asked aloud.

Leonard tapped his index finger on the printout. "Look at the dates. He's been investigating you ever since the PINK incident. It's obvious Fagen thinks you engineered it."

"But that's ridiculous," Kat said. "We saved PINK together. Jack knows how much this system means to me. He would never believe I'd do anything to hurt PINK. He . . . well, he just wouldn't, that's all."

Leonard, however, remained unconvinced. He looked at her over the top of his glasses. "I'm afraid computers don't lie, Ms. Sheffield. If he believes you're guiltless, why is he investigating you behind your back? I know you're somewhat . . . taken with him," he said, tactfully alluding to the looks he, Jenny, and apparently everyone else had seen, "but it's possible he's fostering the relationship just to put you off your guard. He wants you to trust him."

He leaned closer and added, "I believe that Mr. Gates used a similar strategy."

Storm's brewing, thought Jack as he looked out across the garden at the darkening sky. From his vantage point at the French windows, he could see the ominous clouds rolling in from the ocean, as tossed and tangled as the garden below. The air was honey heavy with flower scents and humidity, and still hot with the remembered heat of the day. He shifted uneasily against the door frame, feeling as taut and tight as a drumhead. There was a storm brewing in him as well.

The hacker was good, damn good. The mind behind PINK's sabotage was more evilly brilliant than any of his superiors had anticipated. Jack had needed every ounce of his nerve and cunning to track the mastermind through the circuits and neural nets of Kat's network—with minimal results. Yet the only thing he'd really accomplished was alienating Katrina.

He'd struggled to maintain a coldhearted indifference to her, wanting to keep her as far away from this ugly business as possible. Now he'd even screwed that up.

He'd broken every rule in the book by sending her that necklace, a foolishly sentimental gesture that could compromise his entire operation if he wasn't careful. It could compromise him personally as well. His infernal wanderlust, the one trait of his worthless father he couldn't shake, was already pressing him to move on. In a few weeks he'd be heading on to his next job, leaving Miami—and Katrina—behind.

He frowned, worried that she was beginning to get under his romance-immune skin in a big way. He hated deceiving her, even if it was necessary for both her safety and the safety of his operation. She was one tough lady, but Jack knew that beneath her no-nonsense exterior beat a brave, vulnerable heart. She was such a fragile creature, so trusting, so helpless, so—

"Fagen! Where the hell are you?"

Well, maybe not that helpless, Jack thought as he turned and saw Katrina stalking through the garden. He watched for a moment, enjoying the sight of her struggling against the undergrowth, not to mention the way her skirt hiked up when she stepped over a fallen branch. Apparently she hadn't received his peace offering and was still angry with him. He smiled, thinking she looked more than ever like a kitten on a tear. He lifted his hand and called out. "Still avoiding the front door, I see."

"I knocked, but no one answered," she said as she turned in his direction. She made her way through the jungle and stopped at the bottom step of the terrace, hands on her hips, looking lethal. "You've got some explaining to do, mister. I know what you've been up to."

She knows, he thought, surprised at the relief he felt. At least he wouldn't have to lie to her anymore. "How did you find out?"

"Leonard displayed your transactions and discovered you were investigating me."

She hadn't found out a thing. He rubbed his beard, wondering if the hacker had seen the transactions and jumped to the same wrong conclusions. He hoped so. "Oh, that."

"Yes, *that*," she said, barely containing her fury. She'd expected him to be evasive, or apologetic.

During the drive over, she'd prepared herself to handle either response. But he acted as though he didn't even care, which made her all the more furious. "How dare you pretend it doesn't matter? I trusted you. I thought you meant it when you said you had faith in me."

"I did. I do." He walked down the steps and put his hands on her shoulders. "Look, you've got this all wrong."

She shrugged aside his hands. "The only thing I've got wrong, Mr. Fagen, is believing you could be trusted." She stalked past him up the steps and walked over to the far edge of the terrace. In the distance she heard the rolling roar of thunder, but it was nothing compared with the turmoil inside her. Once again she'd let a man into her heart, and once again she'd gotten hurt. Same story, except that Jack's betrayal was ten times worse than Preston's. No, a hundred times worse. A thousand.

The multiplying stopped when Jack came up behind her, standing so close she could feel his breath stirring her hair. "Kitten, I'm going to tell you something I shouldn't," he said gently. "I was investigating you to prove you *didn't* do it. Someone used your log-on to sabotage PINK. I saw it on the screen that night. That's who I'm after. Not you."

"Someone used my . . ." Kat paled at the implications. Someone in her organization was undermining her systems. One of her own people! Her safe and stable world tilted on its edge. She clasped her arms around her middle, sick inside. "Why didn't you tell me this before?"

Jack brushed a feather-fine strand of hair from the nape of her neck, making her shiver. "I didn't want you involved in this."

The shivering stopped. She spun to face him, her hands balling in rage. "You didn't want me *involved*? Someone is messing with my system and signing my name to it. How much more involved can I get?"

"Okay, maybe I should have told you," Jack acknowledged. "I'm used to working alone, and old habits die hard. Besides, you don't have to worry anymore. Today I found evidence that proves you're innocent."

"Well, bully for you. I suppose it never occurred to you to *ask* me if I was innocent? If you honestly believed I was blameless, you would have asked for my help. Admit it, Jack. You suspected me."

He drew his mouth into a thin, tight line. Lightning flashed behind her and glinted in his eyes, like light off a cold steel blade. "It's my job to suspect everyone," he said, his words sounding as dull and rusty as junkyard metal.

She looked up at his hard-edged features, at the planes and angles she knew as well as she knew her own. Jack's face had invaded her dreams every night for weeks, yet suddenly she felt as if she were looking at a stranger. She wanted her friend back, the wonderful man whose belief in her had helped her to believe in herself. The man she'd come to care for more deeply than even she'd thought possible. But now she realized that that man had been an illusion, a creation of this coolheaded, coldhearted impostor.

God, why did it have to hurt so much?

She had to get out of here. Now. She brushed by him and headed through the French doors. "See you at the office, Mr. Fagen," she said, hoping she sounded more composed than she felt. "And don't worry. Your secret is safe with me."

He followed her into the house. "Katrina."

She turned, unable even now to resist his voice. It was impossible not to remember the last time they'd stood like this, on that sultry night when she'd been drawn to his power like a moth to a flame. So much had happened since then. They'd walked on the beach, they'd shared childhood stories. He'd given her a shell necklace that she wore over her heart. They'd laughed, and fought and made up again with kisses that still burned her lips. Yet the man she'd laughed with and fought with and loved—yes, *loved*—had never been real at all. She ached inside, and knew it was only a matter of time before that ache dissolved into tears. Again she turned to go.

"Kat, I can't let you leave like this."

An hour ago Katrina might have believed that the rough sincerity she heard in his voice was more than a calculated act. Not now. "What's the matter? Afraid I'm on my way to sabotage the system?"

Jack muttered a sharp, emphatic oath. "Look, be practical. I know you want to stop the hacker as much as I do, and now that you know the situation, you can help me. This guy's obviously picked you as his pigeon. The more time you spend accessing the system, the more opportunity he has to incriminate you. If you stay away from work for, say, a week, you'll eliminate that opportunity. I might even be able to catch him red-handed. It makes sense."

Katrina didn't think so. "You want me to desert my system? You want me to leave PINK and Einstein and all the other projects to the mercy of this . . . this criminal?"

"I'll deal with the criminal," said Jack, his dark eyes narrowing. "This guy's no amateur. He's good, and he's dangerous, and he's covering his tracks by setting you up. It'll be easier for me to find him if I'm not worrying about you."

"Thanks for the vote of confidence," she quipped. This was her system they were discussing, for chrissakes! She strode back to face him, her temper blazing. "Get this straight, Jack. I'm not giving up my system. Not to you. Not to anyone."

He reached out and grasped her upper arms,

lightly shaking her. "Can't you see I'm trying to help you?"

His touch ignited her senses, burning through her like a chain reaction in a nuclear core. She wanted him now as much as ever, and hated herself for it. He was a heartless, self-serving man who'd played her emotions like a musician plays his instrument. He'd hurt her more deeply than Preston ever had. She wanted to hurt him back. "Get real, Jack. The only person the Terminator has ever helped is himself."

Instantly she realized she'd gone too far. His eyes narrowed dangerously and his nostrils flared, like a lion sniffing fresh game. Sniffing her. Alarmed, she tried to pull away, but his hands held her fast. "So," he said, his voice low and lethal. "You think I only help myself."

Her heart was pounding so hard she thought it would crack a rib. "Let me go," she said, trying not to sound as frightened as she felt.

She didn't succeed. Jack smiled his familiar rakish grin, but without a trace of warmth. *The better to eat you with, my dear.* She swallowed, her mouth dry as dust. "Please. What are you going to do?"

His smile deepened into a more sinister expression. "What do you think?" he murmured. "I'm going to help myself."

"Jack, no," she said, but her words were drowned out as his mouth came down on hers. He ravaged her, plundering her mouth like a ruthless pirate sacking a defenseless ship. He took her, savagely and deeply, drawing her tongue into his own mouth for his pleasure.

She knew she should pull away. There was nothing soft or sacred, or even personal, about his seduction. This was lust, not love, but what her mind knew, her body ignored. She pressed against him, wantonly encouraging his arousal. She bent back her head, offering her neck to his consuming lips. She felt as if she were in the heart of a tornado, driven by raging elemental forces she couldn't control. She couldn't fight and she couldn't run. She could only survive.

Jack's hand slipped inside her blouse and cupped her breast. His rough fingers stroked the sensitive peak, hardening it instantly. She bit back her gasp of pleasure, struggling to keep a last vestige of self-respect. That vestige dissolved when he lowered her to the couch, and let his mouth complete what his fingers had started.

She was dying by inches. Part of her hated herself for what she was letting him do, but she couldn't stop. He opened her blouse and devoured her with his tongue, his teeth, and his burning eyes. He shifted her beneath him, fitting her to him until the only thing separating them was a few thin layers of material. He rubbed against her, expertly teasing her passion into a fever pitch. Her center ached for him. Jack was a drug and she was addicted, and the only thing she wanted in the world was for him to make love to her.

But this wasn't love. This was sex, base and shallow, and unworthy of deeper feelings she wanted to share with him. They'd couple like two animals in the woods, and when it was over, they'd go their separate ways, emptier and more alone than before. She knew that causing such emptiness in him was a pain she couldn't bear. "Jack," she breathed, her voice hardly a whisper, "I can't. . . ."

She wanted to say "I can't do this to you," but she had no strength left for the rest of the words. Holocaust passion incinerated her reason, leaving only carnal hunger behind. Beaten, she closed her eyes, and gave herself up to the inevitable.

Then, suddenly, he drew away. She opened her eyes and looked up at him, wondering if this was another part of the game. His eyes held a haunted expression she'd never seen in them before. Slowly he reached down, and touched the shell that lay between her breasts.

His touch was soft as a whisper, full of all the gentleness missing in his former lovemaking. Her heart almost broke with its sweetness. Too soon it was over. He pushed himself up and off the couch, and went over to look out the window.

"You'd better go," he told her.

Katrina sat up and curled her hand around the shell. It was still warm from Jack's touch. She didn't want to leave. Not now. "Jack, I—"

"Go, Kat," he said, harsh and raspy. "Go before something happens that we'll both regret."

Regret? Is that all she was to him, a *regret*? A moment ago she thought he honestly cared for her, but he wanted sex, not involvement. He certainly didn't want the friendship she'd thought this necklace symbolized. And certainly not love.

Once again she'd let a man use her, and that knowledge made her blush with shame. She stood up, pulled her blouse and what was left of her dignity around her, and quietly exited the room. She didn't turn back to see if he was watching; she didn't care. Everything she'd ever heard about the heartless Terminator was true. The man wouldn't know an honest emotion if it ran over him in a semi.

She hurried to her car, heedless of the rain that was beginning to fall. The drops fell on her cheeks, mixing with her tears of frustration. She bent down to open her car door and felt the faint swing of the shell necklace against her blouse. Deliberately she reached up and grasped the shell, and yanked it from around her neck. She dropped the broken chain to the ground, slipped into her car, and drove away into the gathering violence of the storm.

SIX

After a warm shower Kat slipped into a white silk kimono robe (one of her recent ridiculous purchases) and settled into an old armchair with a mug of hot camomile tea. In the past she'd used this ritual to soothe her nerves, usually with success. This time, however, it wasn't her nerves that troubled her. And no amount of tea or comfort could ease the desperate hurt inside her.

"Hey, what's shaking?" a familiar mechanical voice said.

Kat looked over at the makeshift computer console she'd set up on her dining-room table. Since the attempted abduction of PINK, she liked to keep a watchful eye on her system day and night. And Einstein, bless him, had taken to keeping a watchful eye on her too. She set her mug on the coffee table. "I'm feeling kind of down."

"Down?" Einstein said, his camera lens zooming in for a close-up. "Babe, you look subterranean. Want to rap?"

Kat shrugged. "There's not much to tell, E. I trusted someone. And that someone turned out to be a lying snake in the grass."

"You talked with snake?"

Despite her gloom, Katrina couldn't help smiling. "Not a real snake. Sometimes you call people snakes when they're cheats and liars, when they sucker you into believing they're the most decent, most honest, most wonderful person you've ever met, only to find they never cared about you at all." She reached down and fingered the sash of her robe. "Sometimes it's an insult to snakes."

Einstein's internal processors clicked. "PINK and I scanning known personality profiles for match on person-snake. No match."

Katrina twisted her sash into a tight knot. "Try Jack Fagen."

"Did. No match."

Kat rose out of her chair. "Well, try again, because that's what he is—a lying, heartless snake who doesn't care about anyone but himself."

Einstein dutifully rechecked his calculations. "Still no match. Employee Personality Test indicates strong defensive mechanism frequently activated to shield sensitive inner emotions. Inability to verbalize emotional states, especially most basic ones. Intrinsic honesty. Conclusion: volatile nature offset by deep-rooted integrity."

Katrina wondered what E would make of Jack's recent display of his "volatile nature" on his living-room couch. Instantly she knew she'd made a mistake. Images of their encounter came to mind—hot, hard, and arousing. Sharp longing shot through her abdomen at just the memory.

How could she be so totally turned on by someone she couldn't stand?

Forcibly she shook the memories from her mind. "I don't care what your profile says, E. He investigated my system transactions."

"I know. PINK helped him."

"PINK," she said incredulously. "He recruited PINK to help get dirt on me? I'll kill him!"

Einstein's camera whirled. "Mortality reference misplaced. Jack used PINK to gather evidence of guiltlessness. He maintained your innocence, even when PINK calculated high probability of guilt."

"Jack thought I was innocent?" she said in a hushed voice.

"If I'm lyin', I'm dyin'."

Katrina frowned. If Einstein was right, Jack had gone out of his way to prove her innocence, despite apparent evidence to the contrary. That didn't support her image of Jack as a lying, backbiting snake.

Still, intelligent computers could make errors in judgment just as people could. Einstein had been known to make mistakes before.

But not often.

Confused, Kat picked up her tea mug and took a sip. Its contents had grown cold—like so many other things in her life. "Einstein," she called over her shoulder as she headed into the kitchen, "take my word for it. Jack Fagen's no good, and he'll come to a 'no good' end."

"Affirmative."

Katrina had picked up the teapot to refill her mug, but paused at E's comment. "Affirmative? Affirmative what?"

"Affirmative Fagen will come to 'no good' end. Profile extrapolation points to increased isolation and accelerating loneliness. Eventual suffocation of all joy and happiness. Prognosis poor."

Katrina put down the teapot, her mug unfilled. "Are you sure? Maybe you've made a mistake?"

"Never make mistakes," Einstein said grandly. "Got to go. Sale on Shopping Channel. Catch you later."

"Bye. And no purchases without permission."

"Aw, you're no fun," E complained, and signed off.

After Einstein had gone, Katrina finished pouring herself a mug of tea, but she never drank it. She stared absently at the amber liquid and heard E's dark words play over and over again in her mind. *Accelerating loneliness. Suffocation of joy. Prognosis poor.* She'd seen the seeds of isolation already growing in Jack. He was a master at shutting people out of his life. E's dire predictions were well on their way to coming true.

Katrina wasn't a fool. She knew Jack was probably twice the liar and opportunist she supposed him to be. But he was also the man who had gone out of his way to prove her innocence, in spite of PINK's probability predictions. He wasn't all bad.

Just mostly.

Annoyed by the direction her thoughts were taking, Kat turned her mind to other things. She straightened the living room, though it hardly needed it. She picked up a book, but got bored in the first chapter. She started to watch TV, but all the shows looked and sounded alike. Despite her efforts, her thoughts kept returning to Jack. Finally she turned to her mail, sifting through the bills and advertisements for something of interest.

A letter from her bank caught her eye. She opened it, thinking it was probably either an account statement or a pitch for a new credit card. It was neither. Inside was a letter of confirmation for the large wire-transaction deposit she'd made earlier that week. It was a fairly straightforward letter, except for one small detail.

Katrina had never made that deposit.

She couldn't breath. Suddenly she was back in the courtroom, listening to Preston's lawyer twist innocent truths into dirty, damning lies. Lies were so much easier to believe than the truth. Past overlay present. No one would believe that she hadn't made that deposit. She'd have to go to court, hear her intimate personal life dissected by strangers. They'd probably ask her about Preston.

Kat, you're overreacting, she told herself. She squared her shoulders and walked to the kitchen to make another cup of tea, but found she could barely hold her hand steady to pour the water. The walls of the kitchen began to close in on her, suffocating her. Just as Preston's lies had suffocated her . . .

She needed air. She threw on a pair of jeans and an old T-shirt, grabbed her purse, and headed out the door. The night air, thick with humidity from the recent storm, tightened around her like a noose. She jumped in her car and started to drive, just drive. She felt like a fly caught in a web, waiting for the spider to strike. A faceless, nameless spider. The thought of going to court again terrified her. She felt frightened, helpless, and alone.

No. Not alone. As she turned her car down a narrow, tree-lined road, she realized she'd unconsciously driven to the estate where Jack was staying. Guided by a hunted animal's instinct to find safe ground, she pulled up to the iron gate and pushed the button for house intercom. She pushed it several times before getting a response.

His voice was sleepy and surly, like a grizzly woken from his winter nap. She didn't care. Surly or not, it was the voice she needed to hear.

She leaned toward the intercom. "Jack," she said shakily, "I need your help."

Jack opened the door to the upstairs spare bedroom and switched on the light. "You can stay in here. I don't want you driving around anymore tonight. Frankly you shouldn't have been driving at all."

She didn't seem to hear him. She walked over and sat down on the bed as if she were in a daze. In her college T-shirt and faded jeans she looked heartbreakingly young and vulnerable, and she clutched her purse to her chest like it was a life preserver. Jack had seen men in battle grip their duffels and backpacks the same way, as if they desperately needed something real to hang on to. It was a symptom of shock. She'd get over it, but Jack wasn't so certain he would. He felt as if she were squeezing his heart.

It's my fault she's going through this, he thought miserably. *If I'd just told her who I was to begin with—*

Her quiet words interrupted his thoughts. "I'm sorry to be so much trouble."

"It's no trouble. I'm glad you came."

Despite her bewildered state, she gave him an incredulous look. "Oh, sure. You don't mind being woken up from a sound sleep in the dead of the night."

Not when you're doing the waking, he thought, but kept that particular sentiment to himself. There were some things she was better off not knowing. She was one of the few decent human beings he'd met in his life. Her trust meant a great deal to him, and he didn't want to take advantage of her.

Not take advantage? He'd practically mauled her on the living-room couch.

He quickly steered away from that potent memory. "I mean it," he said, walking over to the other side of the room. He figured it was wise to put some distance between them. "You could have gone to a family member, or one of your friends."

"Funny," she said, her voice unnaturally calm. "I never thought of going anywhere else. I didn't know what to do. I was just so scared. . . ."

Her voice cracked. *Wisdom be damned*, thought Jack. He closed the distance between them in two steps, then he sat down beside her and gathered her into his arms. "Don't worry, Kitten. Tougher guys than you have cried for far less reason. You're safe now. You don't have to be strong with me."

His words released her. She buried her face in his

chest and cried her heart out. Great aching sobs racked her body, soaking his shirt. Halfway through she realized what she was doing to his clothes and tried to push away. He pulled her back, murmuring words of comfort and reassurance. He held her quaking body, knowing he ought to feel terrible about what she was going through.

He felt wonderful.

Gradually her tears subsided. Her eyes were ringed red with crying, but she looked up at him with a pure, almost childlike trust. Jack had never seen a more beautiful face. "Thanks," she said.

"Anytime," he answered, meaning it. He brushed a strand of silky hair off her forehead. "You're beautiful when you cry."

"Liar," she said, smiling. Then, as if she suddenly realized the provocative position she was in, she sat up and pushed herself away from his chest. "I'm sorry. I didn't mean to make such a spectacle of myself."

"Anytime," he repeated, though his rakish grin gave the word a different meaning.

She tried to laugh at his bravado, but a half-hearted chuckle was all she could manage. She wiped her eyes on her T-shirt sleeve, then clasped her hands tightly in her lap. "Jack, what am I going to do? No one's going to believe that money isn't mine."

"Hush," Jack said, covering both her hands with one of his. "I know you're innocent. We'll find a way to prove it. Together."

Katrina shook her head. "I wish I could believe that. But I know what it's like to be framed. Clever lies are twice as easy to believe as the simple truth, and my past record will count against me." She stared bleakly at the ceiling. "I don't know. Maybe I should just give up and save us both a lot of trouble."

"Trouble and I are old friends," he said, trying to make a joke.

This time she didn't even attempt to laugh. "I appreciate your support, but you're only one person. That's not enough."

Jack looked down and began to stroke the back of her clasped hands with his warm fingers. "Look, Kat, I know how you feel. When I was growing up, I thought the whole world was out to get me. I had a record as long as my arm. My friends, and I use the term loosely, were on the fast track to nowhere. And my mother's only comment was that I was turning out to be a world-class loser just like my dad."

"That's horrible. What did you do?"

He looked up, meeting her eyes. "It wasn't what I did. It was what someone else did."

For a moment Kat wore a puzzled frown, then her face broke out in a radiant smile. *Angels must smile that way*, thought Jack.

"Of course," she said. "Sister Barbara."

"Yes, Sister Barbara. She refused to stop believing in me, even when everyone told her I was no good. Even when *I* told her I was no good. She never gave up on me." He laced his fingers through her own and pulled her over to settle against his shoulder. "All it takes is one person. Just one."

Just one, thought Katrina. She leaned her cheek against his shoulder, drinking in his scent. He smelled of soap and after-shave, and that rich masculine odor that made even the roots of her hair tingle. She burrowed deeper into his warmth. Damn her doubts about him. She needed to feel safe, and the only place she felt safe was in his arms. "Just one person," she breathed, her words brushing like a ghost feather against his neck. "If it's the right person."

Something nuclear happened inside Jack. He looked down at her face and saw absolute acceptance shining in her eyes. Acceptance of him. In spite of his wretched past, his rough nature, and his numerous blunders where she was concerned, she accepted him. It was the most precious gift he'd ever received, and he knew exactly what to do about it. Gently, carefully he lifted her away from his shoulder and got up from the bed. "I'd better leave now," he said, keeping a tight and not altogether successful rein on his voice. "If I don't, we'll probably have a repeat of what happened earlier in the living room."

Kat looked at him with her wide, too-trusting eyes and said softly, "I wouldn't mind."

"I would," he said harshly. He headed out, pausing just once in the door as he left. "You deserve someone better, Kitten," he said over his shoulder. "Better than me."

"I hate satin sheets," Kat grumbled as she shifted uneasily under the covers. The sleek material whispered against her skin like a lover's kiss, inviting seduction—a seduction that wasn't going to happen. Her double bed had a single occupant. The man she'd asked to join her had declined the invitation.

You deserve someone better, he'd told her. Damn fool man. Didn't he know how special he was?

She tossed and turned a few more times, then gave up and got out of bed. She slipped out from the offending sheets and walked to the window, hoping the cool night air would help to clear her mind. It did, but not much. She was still irritated with Jack, but she was beginning to realize that her anger masked a deeper pain.

Preston's rejection had wounded her pride, but Jack's had wounded her heart. She knew in some deep, inexplicable way that Jack needed her as much as she needed him. Yet he'd pushed her away, just as he'd pushed away everything gentle and human in his life.

A night bird cried out and rose into the air. Startled, she looked down into the garden. She thought she saw a shadow moving through the tangled greenery, but it disappeared before she could be certain. Probably a trick of the moonlight, she told herself, or at most a small, harmless animal. She'd found out firsthand how well Jack's security system dealt with larger intruders.

Jack. A sadness she'd never known welled up inside her. How long would it be before loneliness killed all that was caring and decent in him? How many years would it take before his enforced isolation turned him into the machine he was nicknamed for—the Terminator?

Sighing, she looked again at the garden, thinking how cool and peaceful it seemed in the moonlight. *I could stand a little of that peace*, she thought. She needed to get her mind off Jack and onto less disturbing matters. Briefly she considered taking a cold shower, but a last look at the garden changed her mind.

She pulled on her jeans and T-shirt and headed for the bedroom door, glancing at the rumpled bed sheets on her way out. A stroll in the garden might be just the thing she needed to cool her down. *Besides*, she thought ruefully, *I probably wouldn't have gotten much sleep tonight anyway.*

She went downstairs and stepped into the garden, letting its intoxicating magic surround her. Cool peace took a backseat to wonder. Moonlight etched the trees and branches in exquisite silver. Rich, scented air swirled through her mind like exotic incense, reminding her of all the strange and fantastic places her mother had taken her to when she was a child.

But she was no longer a child, and the exotic garden stirred new fantasies in her, fantasies that made her hotter than satin sheets ever could. The smell of damp, fertile loam filled her with primitive energy, and the night wind played like a lover's touch across her bare arms. Nocturnal birds set up an evocative rhythm. Wrapped in the spell of the garden, she swayed to the night's music, letting the fear and frustration flow out of her. She spun around and accidently caught her toe on a hidden root. Crying, she lost her balance and started to fall.

Hands reached out of the shadows and caught her before she reached the ground. Hard fingers grasped her arms, pulling her to her feet. A voice harshly at odds with the night's softness bruised her ears. "Just what in the hell are you doing out here?"

She looked into the cold eyes of her savior. "Jack. I was just . . . out walking."

"Drunken sailors walk straighter than that," he said, scowling. "You should be in bed."

He dropped his hands and stepped back, crossing his arms across his naked chest. Well-worn jeans were the only clothing he wore, jeans that fit him way too close for Katrina's comfort. Heat crackled through her at his nearness, heat coupled with embarrassment at being caught dancing under the moon. She turned away, afraid he'd see her rich blush even in the faint light. "If you don't mind, I think I'll stay out here for a while."

"I do mind." He left the shadows and walked around to block her path. Moonlight glinted off the hard planes of his body like light on metal. "We've got to start tracking down the hacker tomorrow, and I don't want you getting sick on me or fainting from exhaustion."

"Fainting?" Kat said, her temper sparking. "I've never fainted in my life. Stop treating me like a child. I'm as tough as you are, Jack Fagen. And if you had half a brain in that thick head of yours, you'd see . . ."

"See what?" he said, looking sternly down at her.

She took a deep breath, steeling herself for what she was about to say. She tried to sound confident, but her words came out as a whisper. "You'd see I was the best thing that ever happened to you."

He blinked, apparently startled by her boldness. He wasn't the only one. Kat looked down, ready to sink into the ground with embarrassment. *Just once couldn't I leave well enough alone?*

Jack's low chuckle curtailed her dismal thoughts. Surprised, she looked up and saw that his icy eyes had mellowed with soft humor. "You always come out with both guns blazing, don't you, Kitten."

Kat swallowed, completely undone by the warmth in his eyes. This was the man she'd come to care for, the man she couldn't bear to lose again. "I'm trying to be honest, Jack," she said, praying for the words that would open his heart to her. "Please, be honest with me."

She prayed in vain. His eyes grew dark and distant and his mouth pulled into a thin, unforgiving line. "You want honest? I'll give you honest. I'm a hard man living a hard life. People respect me, but they don't like me—and the smart ones don't trust me. If you knew everything about me, you wouldn't trust me either."

"I would," she said. Undaunted, she reached up and gently traced the hard, uncompromising line of his jaw. "I'd trust you with my life."

He groaned aloud and ran his fingers through his unruly copper mane. "Look, Kitten, let me do the decent thing for once in my life. You deserve a better man—"

Kat dropped her hand, her eyes blazing. "I'm getting sick and tired of all this 'better man' stuff. Who do you suggest I hold out for? Ward Cleaver?"

"You don't understand—"

"No, *you* don't understand," she said, her violet eyes flashing. "Last week you rescued PINK from that virus. Tonight, when I was scared to death, you rescued me. You supported me, gave me a place to stay, even gave me a shoulder to cry on. You were there for me. *You*, Jack. And if you're going to stand here and talk yourself down, you . . . well, you can tell it to someone else!"

She spun around and stalked off through the garden, pushing aside the tangled branches with an angry swipe of her hand. Tears ran down her cheeks, but she didn't even bother to wipe them away. It didn't matter. Nothing seemed to matter anymore.

A large cluster of white azaleas blocked her path, stopping her. Bright flowers littered the ground around her feet like stars fallen from heaven, but that didn't matter either. The mystical garden was nothing more than a mishmash of weeds and overgrown shrubbery, uncared for and unloved. Kat hugged her arms tightly to her body, feeling a kinship with the neglected plants around her. The night had lost its magic. A bird called in the distance, sounding plaintive and alone. Her heart echoed its cry.

She heard another sound behind her—muffled

footsteps, quite close. A tiny hope flared within her, but she didn't turn around.

The footsteps stopped. He stood behind her, close enough for her to feel the heat radiating from his body. Close enough for her to smell his darkly masculine scent. "You know," Jack said softly, "you are the most hardheaded woman I've ever met. Except for Sister Barbara, of course."

Kat half glanced at him. His tall form was wreathed in shadows, blacker than the night around him. Unknown. Overpowering. She turned away, suddenly shy. "I've never been compared to a nun before. I'm not sure I like it."

"Then how about an angel?" he said, moving closer. He leaned his cheek against her hair and whispered, "That's what I thought you were when I saw you in this garden. An angel sent from heaven. The answer to a prayer."

"And then I decked you," she said, smiling.

"And then you decked me," he agreed. He circled her with his strong, sure arms and pulled her against him. "First time I've ever fallen for a woman who nearly punched my lights out."

All the love poems in the world couldn't have moved Kat as much as Jack's inelegant words. She shivered in his arms, feeling exquisitely vulnerable, and very frightened. She wanted desperately to make love to him, but he'd had dozens of lovers. She'd had one. He was bound to be disappointed. "Jack. I'm not an angel. I'm only flesh and blood, nothing spec—"

His mouth covered hers, silencing her protests with a deep, searing kiss. His hands roamed over her, incinerating her old insecurities with the loving heat of his touch. She reached up and twined her arms around his neck, pressing herself against the hard, muscled plane of his chest. The passion that had consumed her in the afternoon returned. She gave back his hungry kisses with innocent eagerness, exploring his mouth as thoroughly as his knowing hands explored her body.

Suddenly he stopped kissing her and stepped back. For a paralyzing moment she thought he was going to reject her again. But his gaze was still soft and burning, and his lips held the trace of a smile. "What," he asked, "have you got on?"

She looked down and saw that he'd pulled her T-shirt out of her jeans and up around her breasts. Underneath she wore one of the items of clothing she'd tossed on in her haste to leave her apartment, never giving it a second thought, until now. *The racy red silk teddy.*

"Oh, hell," she said, feeling incredibly foolish. Talk about dressing a sparrow up in cardinal's feathers! She started to pull the T-shirt down, attempting to hide her embarrassment.

Jack's hand clasped her wrist, stopping her. "I'd like to see more," he said, his voice low and husky. He let go of her wrist and hooked his fingers through his belt loops. "Take off your T-shirt."

His words poured through her veins like hot, burning honey. She pulled her shirt over her head, revealing herself to his unwavering gaze. Sensations thick and hot twisted through her, but she struggled to maintain control. She knew her small breasts and too-tall frame didn't turn men on. Preston's luke-warm responses to her body had made that all too clear.

"Now take off the rest."

She kicked away her shoes and slowly stepped out of her jeans. She wished she knew what he was thinking, but it was impossible to read anything from his indifferent stance and his darkly hooded eyes. She shifted uneasily, the cool silk whispering against her sensitive, too-hot skin. Fragile and unsure, she crossed her arms self-consciously across her breasts.

"No." The word was almost a plea. He stepped forward and laced his fingers through hers, pulling her hands away. "Don't hide yourself. You're . . . incredible."

"I am?"

He smiled richly at her disbelief. "Yeah," he said. He lifted one of her hands to his lips and placed a moist, searing kiss on her tender palm. "Oh yeah."

The desire in his eyes ripped her raw. She shuddered, her blood turning molten. He made her new with every phrase, every word, every touch. She drew strength from his strength, pleasure from his pleasure. Passion from his passion.

A new boldness filled her. "Um, I think, maybe, you should take off your jeans."

He arched his brows, surprised and amused by the tentative command. "You sure?"

With this crazy heat pouring though her, she wasn't sure of anything. Except that she wanted him. God, how she wanted him! "Yes," she said as steadily as she could manage. "I'm sure."

He let go of her hands and unfastened his jeans, peeling them off in a few quick moves. She watched his actions with exemplary composure—until she realized he wasn't wearing anything underneath. He tossed aside the jeans, confidently at ease with his nakedness. Kat swallowed, unable to believe that any man could be so muscular, so arousing, gloriously and devastatingly *male*. Lacking experience, she'd assumed that one man's anatomy was basically interchangeable with another's.

Wrong assumption.

As she watched, Jack bent down and pulled a foil packet from the pocket of his discarded jeans. She swallowed again—hard. "Do you . . . always carry those?"

Jack's smile softened. "Ever since my misspent youth. Sister Barbara had definite views on how gentlemen should treat ladies. I doubt the Pope could have talked her out of them."

Kat barely heard his last sentence. *Ladies*, she thought bleakly. *How many had there been? Dozens? Scores? How much accumulated sexual experience did that add up to?*

She mentally calculated the fifteen-odd years he'd been traveling, times three hundred sixty-five days—and nights. Collectively they added up to disaster. Who was she trying to kid? She'd barely been able to satisfy Preston's tepid sexual needs. How could she hope to meet Jack's virile demands? Just looking at him overwhelmed her. A chasm of experience separated them, growing wider with each beat of her aching heart. She turned away. "It's no use," she said miserably. "I'm not experienced like your other lovers. I won't be able to give you . . . what you need."

Jack didn't waste time on an answer. He reached out and grabbed her arm, pulling her roughly against him. His gentleness was gone, replaced by a raw, consuming hunger that burned in the depths of his eyes. He pressed her against the length of his hard, taut body, forcing her to acknowledge his arousal. "I need *you*," he growled, his voice harsh with desire.

His fingers skimmed up her body to her cheeks, igniting the skin he touched.

He held her face close to his, his tight, shallow breath scorching her cheek. "Please—" he began, and stopped as desire momentarily overwhelmed him. He took a ragged, painful breath and began again. "Please don't go."

Aroused as he was, she knew he would let her go if she wanted it. The choice was hers. She could walk away, keeping her pride, and find herself a safer, less demanding relationship. Or she could risk herself for Jack. She was less sure than ever that she could fulfil him, but the depth of his need made her know she had to try. She met his eyes, rocked but not frightened by the devouring heat she saw in their blue depths. "I'll stay."

For a moment she wasn't sure he'd heard her. He didn't move but stood still as stone, watching her with his heavy-lidded, bright burning eyes. An unbearable pressure began to build in her abdomen, torturing her already raw and tender center. She shifted uncomfortably and flickered her tongue over her swollen lips. Jack's gaze fastened on that sudden movement like a hawk spotting prey. His mouth swooped down, capturing her lips with a hot, tangled caress of teeth and tastes and whispered moans. He pulled her tongue into his mouth, kissing her so hard she forgot to breathe. So hard she forgot how to breathe.

New feelings swelled inside her, pouring through her veins like rivers of sweet, crazy fire. She was drowning in them, spinning out of control in the whirlpool her body had become. If a kiss did this to her, what would happen when . . . ? She backed away, suddenly frightened. "Jack," she gasped. "It's too fast. I can't—"

"Hush," he whispered, his eyes softening. His sure hands stroked her neck and shoulders, gentling her like a skittish colt. "There are no can'ts here. I want you, Kitten, not some practiced pleasure doll. I want the things only you can give."

His words and the rhythm of his hands soothed her. "What things are those?"

He smiled, charmed by the simple honesty in her tone. "Your laughter," he said, grazing the ripe fullness of her lips. "Your strength," he added, his mouth exploring the firm softness of her shoulder and upper arm. He paused and raised his head, looking deeply into the velvet glory of her eyes. "And your heart," he said roughly.

He lowered his head and kissed the dark valley between her breasts. She gasped with startled pleasure. He felt her shudder in his arms, a shudder that passed through his own body like an earthquake.

Deep, deep inside him, something essential burned to life. He moved his mouth to her breast, suckling and tasting her through the thin silk of her teddy. Her peak grew rigid under his tongue and his playful nips. Only when she cried aloud did he draw away.

"Lord," he moaned, his words strangled with passion. "I'm sorry, Kitten. You're new to this and I—"

He got no further. She buried her fingers in his hair and pulled herself against his chest, angling her body in a maneuver that sent fire exploding through him. The smile in her eyes told him she knew exactly what she was doing to him. *New, hell*, he thought. The lady could give lessons. Smiling back at her, he lowered his muscular arms to her thighs and gave her a lesson of his own.

Minutes later she lay gasping against him, destroyed by the devastating tenderness of his touch. "You did it again," she said breathlessly. "You searched me without asking."

He rubbed his cheek against her hair, drinking in the smell of her, the hot, heady scent that came from their loving. "Last time I did that you told me to go to hell."

"I did, didn't I." She laughed. The deep throaty sound made his whole body grow taut.

Suddenly it wasn't a game anymore. His need for

her stripped him raw, cutting deeper and stronger than anything he'd felt in his life. He wanted her, and not just physically. "What would you tell me now?"

She sensed the change in him and lifted her gaze to meet his own. Starlight pooled in his eyes, shards of brightness in his hard, uncompromising face. More than anything she wanted to soothe the weariness in that face, to give him some of the joy he'd given her. Love poured through her like a torrent. She raised her hands and lovingly cupped his cheeks. "I'd still tell you to go to hell. But this time," she added, her heart overflowing with love, "this time I'd go there with you."

A long, ragged sigh escaped him. He swept her up in his arms like a weightless doll and started to carry her toward the house.

"No," she whispered thickly. "I want it to be in the garden. Where we met."

He didn't answer. His only verbal response was a low, guttural sound that was cut short when he kissed her. He set her down, letting her slide along the length of his body, feeling every hardened inch of him. Her strength dissolved somewhere during the downward slide, so that by the time her feet touched the ground she was limp as a rag doll.

Jack's sinew-and-steel arm supported her easily. Just as easily he stripped off her teddy, letting it fall in a silken whisper to her feet. Still supporting her, he leaned her back against a nearby tree. The rough bark on her sensitized skin heightened her arousal to a fever pitch.

"Jack," she said, or tried to. The exquisite torment raging through her body made talking, even breathing difficult. The torment increased as his hand covered her breast, stroking its taut, rigid peak with a maddening slowness. Love and lust mated within her to birth a new emotion—beautiful, magnificent, and totally out of control. Every part of her seemed ready to burst with need. Unable to take much more, she settled back against the trunk and, with a maddening slowness of her own, opened her center to him.

Jack's hand stilled. His eyes darkened to a glittering cobalt, transformed by a wonder she'd never expected to see on his hardened face. A lone thought surfaced through the haze of her passion-fogged mind. No one's ever given herself to him like this before, she realized. *This is new for him, too*.

Then he entered her, and thinking lost its attraction.

Silently Jack cursed himself. He'd meant to love her slowly, to give her the most pleasure possible before taking his own in her body. Then she'd parted her legs and his plan became history. Ancient hunger rose in him like a tidal wave, pounding his legendary iron restraint into metallic dust. He needed to be inside her, to know how deep she could take him, to ravish her below as thoroughly as his tongue ravished her sweet mouth above. Instinct drove him—he couldn't have stopped if he tried. A deep, primal rumble of pain and passion escaped his throat. He deftly positioned her body and entered her in a single thrust.

She cried out and clung to him, burying her face in his neck. Cursing aloud this time, he tried to withdraw. She wouldn't let him. Instead she curled her legs around him, drawing him deeper into her tight, mercilessly vulnerable warmth.

"Kitten," he said, struggling to shape the words, "I don't want to hurt you."

She shook her head, her hair brushing his ear and tangling with his own. "You can't," she whispered. "I need this. Much as you do."

"Not possible." He laughed, though it came out as more of a bark. He was fast reaching the point where speech became impossible.

"Is too," she stated, her breathing rough and raspy. She tightened her hold around his neck, as if she thought he might try to dislodge her, despite her protests. "I need this. I need . . . us."

After that confession no power on God's earth could have made him give her up.

The two of them still joined, he lowered her to the ground, unable to give up even a moment of her fisted heat. They tangled together in wild dance, as lush and primal as the garden around them. She made soft, animal sounds when he moved inside her, exciting him more than words ever could. He took her mouth with hard, ravenous kisses—as if her lips were food and water and he was dying of starvation.

Raw passion tore at him like a raging beast. Always before when he'd made love he'd held some part of himself back, afraid to admit the depth of his inner emptiness. But with Katrina even that small restraint was impossible. He poured the whole of his strength into loving her. Impossibly she wanted everything he had to give, accepting him in every imaginable way.

She writhed beneath him, crazy with need. He watched as passion pulled her inside out, and saw her eyes burn like the blue in the heart of a star. He'd never made that kind of beauty in a woman before. He wanted to make her burn again, but his body had other plans. The beast that had been driving him finally overpowered him, ripping him apart in a shattering, glorious instant.

He fell to the soft ground beside her, spent beyond measure, barely able to do more than breathe in the smell of the flowers, the rich loam, and the raw scent of their loving. Exhaustion pulled him toward unconsciousness, but with the last of his strength he reached out and pulled her to him, cradling her against his warmth through the rest of the dark, velvet night.

SEVEN

Dawn was just beginning to steal the stars from the sky when Katrina opened her eyes. Warm and content, she ran her fingers lightly across the midnight-blue sheets of Jack's bed, where they'd moved from the garden sometime during the night. Once here, they'd made love again, less frantically than before, taking the time to explore each other's bodies in a hundred deliciously erotic ways. He had, she'd concluded after a lengthy examination, a magnificently beautiful body. She'd told him so and he'd growled darkly, saying that "magnificently beautiful" didn't sound very macho. He proceeded to show her, in great detail, how extremely macho he was.

All things considered, she'd gotten precious little sleep last night. And had a fantastic time doing it. Sated and sleepy, she leisurely untangled herself from the night-hued covers. "I *love* satin sheets," she said, yawning.

"I'm more partial to what's in those sheets," Jack said, deep laughter rumbling in his chest. He reached out and brushed an unruly curl from her forehead, his rough-cut fingers impossibly gentle. "Morning, Kitten."

His voice was soft and reverent, like a prayer. Kat's heart swelled inside her, aching with almost unbearable pleasure. It seemed that all her life she'd been waiting for someone to say "Morning, Kitten" in just that way. "Morning," she answered, matching his reverence. And then, just to keep things in perspective, she added, "You snore."

"Do I?" he said, grinning. "Well, that's your tough luck." He drew back his hand and raised himself on his elbow, looking down at her. His hot gaze wandered over her with undisguised appreciation. "You sure wake up pretty."

"I'm a mess," she argued self-consciously. "My eyes are puffy and my hair's a disaster."

Inwardly Jack groaned. *Women. Why did they always equate neatness with desirability?* "You are, hands down, the most beautiful, most tantalizing, most sexy woman I've ever had the pleasure to wake up with. And if I didn't think it'd endanger my health, I'd prove it to you."

"Really?" she whispered. "You really think I'm sexy?"

Jack made a sound of exasperation. "Good Lord, after last night you have to ask? Kitten, the earth moved. It's never been like that for me before."

Kat caught her breath. Vivid scenes of their passionate lovemaking bombarded her mind. Bold and primitive, Jack had introduced her to the intoxicating joys of loving and being loved in return. Yet he was also a generous and giving lover, helping her to rediscover the desires she'd kept hidden away since the trial, afraid to trust her feelings again. With Jack she wasn't afraid to be totally and completely herself, a freedom she'd never shared with any man, including Preston. If that didn't qualify as "earth-moving," she didn't know what did. "I guess that makes two of us," she whispered.

Life's sweetest pleasure, she decided, was waking up in the bed of the man you loved. Relaxed, radiating happiness, she stretched like a contented cat. Her hand slipped lazily under the pile of satin pillows and unexpectedly brushed something coolly metallic. Puzzled, she closed her fingers around the small object and drew it out.

It was her shell necklace.

She sat up and held the chain between her hands. "Jack, you saved it," she said, delighted. "That's so sweet."

"Sweet," he groaned, falling back into the piled pillows. "People on three continents quake at the sound of my name, and you think I'm sweet. You're going to ruin my reputation."

His remorse over his crumbling macho image made Kat love him all the more. She twined the chain through her fingers, wondering if he had any idea how much this gesture meant to her. Even after their terrible fight and his apparent rejection, he hadn't given up caring about her. It must have hurt him deeply to see her throw away his gift. She looked down, ashamed of her childish actions. "I'm sorry I broke this. If I'd yelled less and listened more—"

Jack's larger hand gently grasped hers and pulled it against his heart. "You had ever right to be angry. I wasn't being honest with you. I'm the one who should apologize."

She buried her fingers in the soft, warm fur of his chest. "You're being honest with me now. That's all that matters."

Was it her imagination, or did his muscles tense at her words? Worried that she'd somehow managed to hurt him again, she bent closer. "Jack, is something wrong?"

A vulnerability crept into his eyes, dramatically at odds with his rough, rugged features. Whatever the cause, she longed to ease the tension in him, to smooth out the careworn furrow between his craggy brows. Gently she stroked his furred chest, feeling the strong and steady beat of his heart underneath.

His expression changed, becoming anything but careworn. His breath quickened, and a low, almost feral growl emerged from the back of his throat. Kat's hand stilled. She felt the hair rise on the back of her neck, and wasn't sure she disliked the feeling. "Jack?"

"Oh, to hell with my health," he growled, rising up and covering her body with his own.

Living heat leaped between them. He lowered his mouth to the hollow at the base of her neck, searing her with his hot, demanding lips. Katrina gasped, experiencing anew the sweet, sacred burning that had consumed them both last night. It wasn't just sex. Giving herself to Jack, making love with him, was changing her in ways too profound and elemental to name. She knew that she would carry some of his strength and courage with her for the rest of her life, even after he'd caught the hacker who was sabotaging her system and gone on to his next job.

Even after he'd gone.

Kat stiffened, caught off guard by the thought. She shouldn't be surprised. She'd always known Jack would be leaving when his job was over. He'd made that clear from the start—

Jack stopped kissing her and lifted his head. His

eyes met hers with a quizzical look. "What's wrong?"

"Nothing," she said, trying to sound natural. She couldn't meet his eyes, knowing he'd see the painful thoughts reflected in her gaze. He knew her that well. "Nothing at all."

Jack didn't buy it. He rolled off her and lay beside her, his head propped on his hand. "Katrina, last night didn't leave many secrets between us. I know you're the kind of woman who makes love with her mind as well as her body, but right now your thoughts are a million miles away. Now what's the matter?"

"I . . . I was thinking about the guy who made the deposit," she said. It wasn't entirely a lie.

Jack's expression softened. He reached out and smoothed her soft, tousled hair. "Ah, Kitten, don't worry about that. I'm not going to let anything happen to you. I'll catch the hacker. Truth is, he's not such a smart guy after all. If he were, he wouldn't have made that deposit into your account."

"But that deposit implicates me."

"It implicates him, too," Jack explained. "That letter from the bank said that the deposit was a wire transfer, which means that there's a computer record of where it came from. And if we find out *where* the money came from—"

"We'll know *who* it came from," Katrina finished. "But, Jack, the bank might not keep that information on their files. If they don't—"

"If they don't, we'll figure out something else. I told you, Katrina. I'm not going to let anything happen to you. That's a promise."

A promise. Unexpected tears pricked her eyes. Bravery came in many forms, she realized. Jack's background had made distrust a way of life for him. His belief in her, despite his training, took a special kind of courage. "Jack, I want you to know that whatever happens, I—"

"Hush," Jack said, moving his hand from her hair to her mouth. He brushed his fingertips over her sensitive lips, his touch as intimate as any caress. He leaned closer, a hint of desperation in his eyes. "The night's almost over, Kitten. Let's not waste what little time we have left on words."

She nodded, filled with a desperation of her own. Jack's tender passion had shown her what loving really meant, the acceptance of the most intimate, vulnerable part of herself by another human being. It was a rare and precious gift, and one she ached to return in kind.

She reached out and twined her fingers in his hair, bringing his mouth down to hers. Surprise momentarily flashed in his eyes, until the raw heat of the kiss eclipsed both of their senses. Strength gave to strength as their tongues met in a wild mating dance. His large frame shuddered with pleasure, pleasure she was giving him. His pleasure intoxicated her. Seeking to please him more, she pushed him down and straddled his naked body with her own.

Jack gasped. "Kitten, you're driving me crazy!"

This time it was Kat who grinned rakishly. "Patience, love," she whispered as she moved to ease their mutual need. She and Jack might not have much time together, but they had this moment. They had to share a lifetime of love in this moment, and by heaven, she was going to make every second count.

"Leonard, you don't understa . . . Leonard? Leonard!" Katrina slammed Jack's car phone back into its cradle. "I don't believe it. He hung up on me."

Jack kept his eyes on the road, but the corner of his mouth twitched up. "I take it he doesn't approve of you spending the day with me."

"That's putting it mildly. He thinks I should fire you for daring to investigate me. He thinks I'm being blinded by your, uh, charms."

"Charms?" Jack said, grinning openly at her use of the obviously un-Leonard-like euphemism.

"Well," Kat admitted, "that wasn't *exactly* the

word he used. Leonard's very protective when it comes to the system. I wish I could have told him about the computer hacker."

"Katrina, we can't afford to tell anyone," Jack said. "The more people who know, the more chance the hacker has of finding out and going to ground. Believe me, the less people who know, the sooner we'll catch this jerk."

And the sooner you'll be leaving, she thought bleakly. Emotionally she felt like two separate people—one who wanted the blood of the man who dared mess with her system, and one who died a little each time she realized what his capture would mean. She stole a look at Jack's profile, at the hard, forbidding features that concealed a gentle and loving nature. A bittersweet pain lodged in her heart. Her love, patience, and tenacity had drawn out his vulnerable side. Would anyone care enough to draw it out again?

"We're here," Jack said, turning into the bank's parking lot. He glanced at his watch. "And we made it in record time. I guess the traffic gods were with us."

"They're the only ones who are," she murmured.

Jack looked at her, puzzled by her unnaturally quiet tone. Quiet and Katrina didn't mix. Worried, he looked over at her, noting the slump of her shoulders and the weary tilt of her head. *Poor kid*, he thought guiltily. She'd been through an awful lot in the last few days, more than any nonprofessional deserved. "Look, Kitten, if you're not up to this—"

She laid a hand on his arm and gave him a smile so sweet his heart ached. "We're in this together, Jack. You and me. We'll teach this guy not to mess with us."

Us. The word resonated through his soul. He'd always worked alone, prizing his isolation even on his group assignments. He'd rarely let down his emotional barricades with anyone before. Certainly not with a woman.

Trust wasn't something he gave lightly, but as he got out of the car and walked around to Katrina's side, he realized he'd unconsciously given her that trust long ago. He'd shared more of his inner thoughts and feelings with her than with anyone, including Sister Barbara. He wanted to share a future.

What future? An endless string of rented rooms and rootless wanderings? He couldn't give her a home. He couldn't even give her an address.

He reached Katrina's door and yanked it open. "Let's get moving. The sooner we get this over with, the better."

Better for her, he thought. *Bloody hell for me*.

"It's not our policy to give out that type of information."

Katrina stared incredulously at the bank's customer-service representative. "But it's right there on your computer screen. You just told me it was."

The sharp-jawed woman nodded. "Yes, but we have strict procedures concerning federal clearing-house wire transactions. I'm not authorized to give you that information verbally."

"But it's my account."

The woman gave her a sympathetic but totally uncompromising look. "Please try to understand. Everything's regulated by precise government standards to protect the customer. We're doing this for your benefit."

"Well, I don't feel very benefited," Kat said darkly. She'd just spent twenty minutes waiting to see this representative—twenty of the worst minutes of her life. Jack's mood was downright surly, hurtfully so. It was as if the night before never existed—

"Is that all?" the representative asked, interrupting her thoughts. "Because if it is, I have other people waiting."

"Let them wait," Kat said sharply, fast approaching the end of her tether. She'd spent twenty horrible minutes waiting for this. Jack was counting on her to get the information. She wasn't going away empty-handed. "Look, there must be some way for me to find out where that deposit came from."

"Of course," the woman said. She reached into her desk drawer and pulled out a handful of papers. "Just fill out these forms, in triplicate, and return them to me. I'll be happy to forward them to the research department, and they'll have an answer for you in no more than ten days."

Ten days? In ten days the hacker could be half-way to China, with PINK, Einstein, and the rest of her system projects in tow. She didn't have ten days. Frankly she didn't know if she had ten minutes.

Fuming, Kat scooped up the papers and stalked out of the woman's office. Jack was waiting for her just outside the door. "How did it go?" he asked.

"Like Napoleon at Waterloo," she said as they walked through the crowded bank to the outer lobby. The tinny, falsely bright Muzak only added to her frustration. She'd never lost easily, but this time was worse because she'd failed Jack too. She leaned against the cool green marble of the lobby wall, thinking she'd never felt so useless. "I should have checked with PINK. She'd have told me I didn't stand a chance with these paper pushers. Dealing with bureaucrats is like fighting a punching bag. There's just no way to win."

"Maybe there is," Jack said.

Something in his tone worried her. She looked up and saw that his gaze was fixed on a deserted corner of the bank offices where several pieces of electronic equipment had been stacked against a far wall. A movable partition hid the equipment from the customers, and from most of the bank employees as well. But not, Kat noted, from the armed security guard stationed by the lobby door. "Jack, what are you up to?"

"This computer system is set up on a LAN," Jack said, using the acronym for a network of computer terminals. "I've been studying the layout. The server port is set up in that corner, away from the rest of the terminals. No one is using it. No one's even near it. I can use it to pull up your account records."

She thought he was making a joke, but the determined set of his jaw was anything but humorous. His face held the look of intense concentration of a man figuring out all the angles, like a gambler before a race or a burglar before a robbery. Katrina stiffened. "You can't be serious. The security guard—the armed security guard—isn't going to let you just waltz over and access confidential bank files. Besides, you don't know the bank security log-on code."

"That's not a problem. I have a universal bank access code."

"You have a . . ." Kat began, shock registering clearly on her face. Universal access codes were issued to only a handful of government fiduciary auditors, people with security clearances higher than the ionosphere. "How in the world did you get one?"

For an instant his smile slipped, as if her question caught him completely off guard. She glimpsed another expression underneath, but before she could identify it, it was gone. "Katrina," he intoned, his rakish grin securely back in place. "You don't really want to know how I got the code, do you?"

No, probably not, she thought, considering the only way he could have gotten one was to steal it. Risking a stint in a federal penitentiary wouldn't faze Jack Fagen. She looked into his too-bright eyes, knowing she was seeing a man who'd developed an unhealthy appetite for danger. *Or,* she thought chillingly, *an unhealthy disregard for himself.* "Even if you can get into the computer, you still have to deal with the security guard."

"Not if he doesn't notice me. With all these people around there's a good chance he won't."

"And a good chance he will," she argued. "Look, there's other ways we can do this. We can go back to my apartment and give your code to Einstein. He'll be able to access the files—"

"And leave a transaction trace a mile wide," Jack finished. "Face it, the best way to access the files is from a local terminal."

Kat shook her head. "It's too risky."

"If it is, it's my risk to take!"

In her heart Katrina knew he hadn't meant to sound so harsh. That didn't make it hurt less. "Fine," she said tersely. "Get arrested. Get shot even. I don't care."

His smile softened and his devil blue eyes took on a warmer cast. "Kitten, I'm sorry. I've been on my own for a long time. I'm not used to having someone else . . . worry about me. But you've got to believe that I know what I'm doing. Go outside and wait for me. I'll join you in a few minutes."

He turned to leave, but she grasped his wrist, holding him back. "Jack, don't go. It's too dangerous. Let me help you. Maybe I could distract the guard?"

Jack's indulgent smile alternately thrilled and annoyed her. "Katrina, much as I'd like to play the hero, this isn't all that dangerous." He gently lifted her hand from his arm, raised it to his lips, and gave her pale knuckles a swift, warm kiss. "Wait for me outside."

"Like hell I will," she whispered as she watched his broad form mix effortlessly into the crowd. She wasn't going anywhere. She hadn't believed his reassurances for an instant, and she was desperately worried, despite his obvious skill at blending into the background. He was good, but he was only human. No way was she deserting him.

Kat turned her attention to the security guard.

He was middle-aged and slightly paunchy, but his terrier stance and his spit-shine image announced retired marine corps loud and clear. He didn't look like the kind of man who could be easily distracted by a woman. He didn't look like he'd be distracted by an earthquake.

So what now? she wondered grimly. *Do I faint into his arms? Do I lift my skirt like some gambler's moll in a bad forties movie?* She looked at the guard's relentlessly humorless expression. Neither idea seemed promising.

But they gave her an idea that did.

She walked over to the bank of pay phones in the lobby and dialed a number she'd come to know better than her own. A mechanical click at the other end indicated the connection had been made. "Einstein? Are you there?"

"Natch, babe," returned the electronically modulated voice. "What's shaking?"

My knees for starters, Kat thought, though she didn't relay that information to Einstein. No sense getting his circuits in a tizzy. "E, is PINK still listening in on the radio and wire services for racing information?"

"No way. No how. She isn't. Hasn't done it for weeks."

Despite her tension, Katrina's mouth curled into

a smile. "Now, E," she admonished. "Tell me the truth."

"Well . . ."

Kat's mouth broke into a positive grin. "I'm not going to scold her. I need her help. I want her to find out what radio frequency is playing this," she said, briefly holding the receiver up toward the speaker and its homogenized Muzak. "And after she finds that out, I want her to . . ."

Katrina gave Einstein a short list of instructions. Thankfully he seemed to sense the urgency of the situation and didn't ask his usual battery of crazy questions. A soft whir on the other end of the line told Kat that he was passing the information on to PINK. Waiting, she looked toward the crowded lobby and picked out Jack's large but surprisingly hard-to-spot form. He'd made his way to the far wall and was drifting toward the partition.

Unexpectedly a surge of excitement flowed through her. Watching Jack, she realized nothing she'd done had ever mattered so much before. She'd never mattered so much before. He depended on her. She was his partner, his lifeline, his—

"I'm back, babe," Einstein stated. "PINK's on deck. Ready when you are."

Kat said nothing, clutching the phone in a death grip. Her gaze was fixed on Jack, watching as he reached the edge of the partition. He glanced her way and gave her a ghost of his trademark smile. Kat's heart slammed against her chest. "Now," she whispered into the receiver.

The Muzak sputtered out. Customers and bank employees paused, then went back to their business, unconcerned. The guard didn't even blink. For a tense moment Katrina wondered if E had passed on all her instructions. Then—

The air exploded with sound. Speakers blared a high-volume combination of MTV rap music, the Hialeah Park racing results, and even a sales pitch from the Shopping Channel. People covered their ears, looking at each other in alarm, annoyance, and in some cases amusement. The guard made a beeline for the teller stations and the bank's money, just as Katrina hoped he would. He never looked at the stacked equipment.

Her plan had worked. Amazement washed over her, and as the shock of relief hit her she started to giggle. It was funny watching the unflappable bank bureaucrats run from speaker to speaker like chickens with their heads cut off. The giggle turned to a chuckle and was heading toward a full-fledged laugh when a strong hand grasped her elbow.

"End it now," Jack commanded.

Still chuckling, she lifted the receiver. "That's enough, E. Nice job."

"Piece of toast," Einstein said, signing off.

The riot of sound cut out and was instantly replaced by the carefully modulated Muzak. Expressions of complete dismay crossed the faces of the stupefied bureaucrats. Kat would have enjoyed watching them try to figure out what had happened, but Jack was already hurrying her toward the door.

"Don't ever, ever do that again," Jack said as they burst into the sunlight.

Katrina looked up at his stormy expression, feeling piqued by his anger. "I was only trying to help. Did you get the information?"

"Yes, I got the information. That's not the point," he said as he propelled her across the parking lot. "That was a dangerous stunt you pulled. You could've ended up in prison."

"So could you."

"It's different for me. I'm . . ." He paused and gave her a quick, guarded look. "Listen, it's different for me. I can handle the risk. You can't."

"It was my risk to take," she said softly.

He stopped in his tracks, stunned at the sound of his own words on her lips. "Mother of God. Is that what you felt like?"

Kat nodded slowly. "I didn't mean to upset you. I guess," she added, biting her lip. "I guess I'm not any more used to having someone worry about me than you are."

He looked down at her, anger and wonder chasing themselves across his face. "You know, sometimes I don't know whether to kiss you or strangle you."

"Kiss me first," she suggested, wrapping her arms around his neck. They stood in the middle of a sun-drenched parking lot in downtown Miami, but she couldn't have cared less. Something inexplicable had passed between them, something more important than the deposit information, the hacker, even, God help her, than her system. She pulled Jack's mouth down to hers, completing the connection. Energy and joy poured through her like live electricity, forging something stronger than passion, stronger than life itself. She heard him murmur something about "not standard procedure," then he locked his arms around her and kissed her so hard her knees buckled.

A blaring horn broke their embrace. Kat looked up and saw a car bumper inches from her leg. She and Jack were standing in the middle of the parking aisle, blocking traffic.

Lord, how embarrassing, she thought as Jack's strong arms pulled her aside. "Sorry," she said to a passing Buick.

The driver was an older woman wearing rhinestone glasses and a tolerant expression. "S'okay, honey. If I had a hunk like that, I'd block traffic, too."

Jack chuckled roughly. "A hunk," he commented as they headed toward the car. "The lady has taste."

"And glasses an inch thick," Kat added, trying to counteract the thrill his laughter sent down her spine. They had work to do, a hacker to catch. She needed to keep her mind on business—and off the fact that her days with Jack were numbered.

EIGHT

Katrina looked out of the kitchen pass-through. "Any luck?" she asked.

"No," Jack answered, following the word with a short but highly colorful curse. He set his empty coffee mug down on Katrina's dining-room table and turned back to Einstein's monitor screen. "E, can't you run your search on those files any faster?"

"If could, why would I be processing at lower speed?"

In the kitchen, Katrina bit back a laugh. Humor was not what Jack needed at the moment, especially when he'd spent the entire afternoon sorting through a seemingly endless array of national and international data bases. The bank number he'd gleaned from her deposit record was proving harder to locate than either of them had imagined. She pulled a mug out of the cabinet and poured him some more fresh coffee. He needed her support, not her ridicule. Even if he did look like a giant teddy bear hunched over her dining-room table.

She came out of the kitchen and walked over to Jack, setting the steaming mug down beside him. "Can I help?"

A curt shake of his head was the only response he offered. Kat revised her opinion. More like a grizzly bear.

She knew she should leave him to his work. Instead she found herself leaning against the table, her gaze lingering on his hard-edged profile. Seemingly unaware of her presence, he'd let his usual controlled expression slip, allowing his true feelings to show through. She saw concern there, and a stern frown of intense concentration. But there was another, more disturbing look—a strain around his eyes that spoke of a weariness so intense it bordered on despair. The lines ran deep—carved, she imagined, during the loveless days of his childhood, and chiseled deeper every empty year since then. *Prognosis poor*, she remembered, recalling Einstein's dire prediction. *Oh, Jack, you don't have to be alone anymore.*

An ache rose in her chest for the lonely boy he must have been and the solitary man he'd become. Unbidden, she reached over and carefully pulled out a burnished copper curl that was caught under the collar of his dark polo shirt. If only she could've pulled out his pain that easily. If only—

Her thoughts stopped as he unceremoniously waved away her hand. "Kat, I don't have time for that now."

A deep rose stained her cheeks. "I wasn't—" she began, but stopped. How could she explain the emotions that swirled through her, bright as a magic lantern show? He'd batted away her tender touch as if it were an annoying house fly. She wasn't about to let him bat away her precious feelings too. "Fine," she stated, straightening up from the table edge. "Let me know if you need any cream."

He glanced at the mug, then up at her. "Hell," he said, rising from his chair. "Kitten, I'm sorry."

"I wasn't coming on to you—"

"I know," he said, folding her into his arms. "I was just so wrapped up in my work."

"You didn't have to be mean about it."

"Yeah," he said, sighing. He pulled her close and stroked her silky hair. "I'm a jerk."

Against his chest her mouth pulled into a smile. "Yes, you are," she said, her words muffled. "But I love you anyway."

Jack's body went rigid.

Damn, she thought. *I've used it*. The "L" word. Men didn't like that word. Love implied clinging dependence, commitment, weakness. Even at the height of their relationship Preston preferred her to use more fashionable terms: main squeeze, special fella, significant other. . . .

"You what?"

For a moment she considered lying, substituting a less loaded word. But how could she? How could she deny the truest, most profound emotion she'd ever felt for a man? Loving Jack was as much a part of her as her own name. She raised her eyes, meeting his blue gaze with amazing composure. "Do you mind very much?" she asked.

"I don't know," he said, his voice tight with some emotion, she couldn't tell what. Then the edge of his mouth curved up in a thoughtful smile. "I don't think 'mind' is the operative word."

The soft edge of humor in his voice almost made her wince. He was laughing at her. Well, why not? She'd just blurted out that she loved him, something he'd probably heard from dozens of other women—beautiful, exotic women who could offer him pleasures she couldn't even imagine. When it came to love, she was strictly minor league. Embarrassed, she started to draw away. "I shouldn't have said it. It was dumb. Preston never liked it when I—"

Jack pulled her to him with a force that knocked the wind out of her. "Get this straight," he said, his eyes gleaming dangerously. "I don't give a damn what Preston liked or disliked. I don't even want to hear his name. That clear?"

Kat nodded, too shocked to speak. She'd seen Jack angry before, but never this intense.

Jack continued. "You've got to stop quoting him like his word is gospel. The guy's a—" He paused, searching for a phrase that would sum up Preston's worthlessness. "He's a waste of good protoplasm."

Kat smiled at his use of Einstein's favorite insult. "I know he is. But his opinion matters, or did. He's the only other man I've ever . . . well, I haven't had a lot of experience with men. I suppose that's why it was so easy for him to fool me. I didn't trust anyone for a long time. I didn't know if I even could trust anyone again." She lifted her hand and cupped his bearded cheek. "Then I met you."

"I'm the only other man . . ." he began, his voice oddly unsteady. He lifted his hand to tenderly cover her own. "Kitten, there's something I have to tell you—"

"Got it!" Einstein interrupted. "Found number!"

Katrina's face broke into a radiant smile. "He found it, Jack!" she cried, breaking their embrace and heading back to the computer screen. "Now we're a step closer to putting away that son of a . . ." Her words died out as she read the heading on the top of E's computer screen. "Pentagon? You're reading Pentagon data bases?"

"Hey, one bank file's the same as another," Jack said quickly.

Too quickly, Kat thought, a vague uneasiness growing in her heart. Pentagon files were not just like everyone else's, whatever he said. Jack followed her over to the computer and leaned toward the monitor screen, almost obscuring her view. Almost. She just caught the name of the bank before Jack punched a key and cleared the screen. Grand Cayman National Bank. Grand Cayman.

Her security-trained mind automatically fitted the various puzzle pieces into place, and the picture they formed was far from pretty. She stepped back, rubbing arms that had gone suddenly cold, and looked at the man she loved as if she were seeing him for the first time. Maybe she was. "What's going on here?"

Jack looked up, startled by the hushed desperation in her tone. He gave her his most winning smile. "Nothing. Nothing at—"

"Don't lie to me! Since the Swiss changed their disclosure laws, the Cayman Islands have been the banks of choice for illegal operations worldwide. That, combined with your access to Pentagon files, and your universal bank code . . . You're good, Jack, but no one's that good." She took a steadying breath, trying to stem the pain that flowed through her like a rising tide. "Tell me the truth. Please."

He straightened to his full height, his tall figure looming over her like a dark, imposing mountain. Only his eyes were soft, holding the same sky-blue yearning she'd seen in them the first night. *You were a sucker then too*, she reminded herself. Deliberately she turned away from his eyes. When she turned back, they were as starkly cold as the rest of him.

"All right," he said, his voice as chilling as his eyes. "About six months ago strategic military secrets started showing up in the hands of terrorist organizations. Leads were traced, but they never panned out. Eventually it became obvious that someone on the inside was hampering the investigation. Someone highly placed."

Jack walked over to her couch and sat on the back, crossing his arms in front of him. His lips curled into a mocking smile. "They hired me because they couldn't risk soiling their lily-white political futures with a messy internal scandal. I did their dirty work for them. Using bogus information as bait, I tracked the leak through the international computer networks, through the various shell nodes and shadow systems. It was like trying to find a needle in a haystack, but eventually the trail led me to—"

"Sheffield Industries," Kat finished, her throat

constricting with a familiar pain. "He's using my system as a backdoor. Just like Preston."

"No, not like Preston," Jack corrected. "The Sheffield connection is only a small cog in a very big wheel. But this man can lead us to the organizers. That's why I can't let him get away."

That's why. Not because you wanted to clear my name. "But if that's true, why go to all the trouble to hide it? Like at the bank today. They would have given you the bank number. You could have walked up and flashed your credentials—"

"—and blown my cover sky-high. I couldn't risk it. But remember, I did tell you getting that number wasn't as dangerous for me as you thought."

Kat remembered. She also remembered how proud she'd been of helping him—help he hadn't needed at all. How stupid she must have looked to him. She felt like a fool. "You should have told me."

"Kat, I'm working deep cover. I couldn't risk you accidentally exposing my operation."

"Right. Especially with my past."

"I never believed you were involved."

"But you couldn't be sure, could you?" she accused. She hugged her arms tightly to her body, as if, like a tourniquet, she could somehow cut off the pain. She couldn't. Sorrow bubbled through her like water from a bitter well. Jack's duplicity broke her heart, but she'd be damned if she was going to let him know that. She raised her head and faced him with all the composure she could muster. "Under the circumstances, I think it would be better if you left."

Jack shook his head. "I'm not going anywhere."

"You have the name of the bank. You can find the hacker. There's no reason for you to stay."

His bold gaze raked her body from head to foot. "I can think of several," he said softly.

Her cheeks flamed, the outward sign of a deeper, rising heat. She swallowed, her mouth gone suddenly dry. Appalled, she realized that if he held her, if he even so much as touched her, she'd forget everything and melt into his arms. She wanted him, even though she knew he'd just been using her. God help her, she still loved him.

She willed herself to ignore her feelings. "Stay if you like. I'm sure Einstein can help you to track the hacker, but I've had enough for one evening." She turned and walked toward the back hallway and her bedroom. "Let me know if you need any references, Jack. As your employer I can recommend your work highly. But personally," she added, glancing back at him, "you can go to hell."

She was gone. For a moment he watched the hallway, half hoping she'd reappear and throw herself into his arms, forgiving him. And half hoping she wouldn't. Getting mixed up with him was the worst thing that could happen to a woman like Katrina. Better to end things now before something serious happened.

Right, Jack. Like before she falls in love with you.

He groaned, hating himself for not seeing how inexperienced she was with men, how ready she was to fall in love. Between him and Preston she'd probably never trust herself to love anyone again, and the thought of Katrina living a life as solitary as his own filled him with an almost unbearable anguish. He'd lived on his own since he was a kid. But Katrina had been raised with love. She needed to give love, and be loved in return.

"Aren't you going after her?"

Jack looked up, surprised by the sound of Einstein's voice. He'd forgotten that the computer was still turned on. Apparently E had witnessed everything. "I don't think it would do any good," Jack said, rising wearily from the back of the couch.

"She's mad at you," Einstein stated unnecessarily.

Frustrated, Jack raked his fingers through his hair. "That's an understatement. If she even talks to me again, it will be a minor miracle."

Einstein's video lens whirred, focusing on Jack's face. "Expression suggests dissatisfaction with current situation. Can offer solutions."

Jack's hands dropped to his side. He took a step toward the terminal. "Like what?"

A series of intricate equations flashed across E's screen. "PINK's probability studies indicate best way to reestablish communications is to propose marriage. Has eighty-three-point-six-percent success coefficient."

"Marriage?" Jack said incredulously. "E, you can't propose marriage, just to . . . to 'reestablish communications.' Marriage means a lifetime together, a future. You know the kind of life I lead. There's no way I could guarantee her a future."

"Like, for sure. Empirically speaking, no guarantees for future. For anyone." Einstein retraced his video cam. "So, want another solution?"

"No," Jack said slowly. A thoughtful smile played across his lips. "Einstein, don't let anyone tell you you're just another pretty face."

"Damn straight," E said, signing off.

Jack left the living room and walked down the hallway to Kat's bedroom door, and knocked softly. When he got no answer, he tried the knob. It was locked tight.

He raised his hand and knocked again. "Katrina. Let me in. There's something I want to tell you."

"I don't want to hear it. Go away."

Jack grinned at the fierceness of her muffled reply. His little spitfire was back. "I'm not going away. And unless you want this door in pieces, you'd better open it. I'm coming in. One way or the other."

Moments passed and he began to wonder if he actually was going to have to break the door down. Then he heard movement. The lock turned and the door opened.

"Thanks," he said as he entered.

"You didn't give me much choice," Kat answered sullenly. She moved away to the other side of the room, putting the wide brass bed between them. She looked out the picture window, her back turned. "What do you want?"

I want to see you smile. I want to hear you laugh and see your eyes shimmer like stars dancing. Small chance of that, he thought grimly. Outside her window he could see the ocean darkening into a beautiful indigo evening, full of spice-laden breezes and hushed surf whispers. But she'd shut the window tight against everything except the view, just as she'd shut her heart against everything he needed to say. *Jack-boy, you've got your work cut out for you.* "I know I'm probably one of the last people you want to see right now—"

"Try *the* last," she said, keeping her back to him.

"Look," Jack countered, "this isn't easy for me, either. Right now I'd rather face down a gang of third-world commandos than you."

"Don't let me stop you."

Jack winced as the barb hit home. "Okay, maybe I deserve that. But I was in a spot. I couldn't tell you. You've got to understand, Kitten, I was under orders not to tell anyone."

She clasped her arms around herself and said nothing.

Why didn't she turn around? he wondered. Did she hate him so much she couldn't even stand to look at him? For the first time he realized he might not be able to put things right between them, and the thought twisted through him like a knife. "I never meant to hurt you," he said, his voice rising in desperation. "You've got to believe that."

Still nothing. Her silence added another brick to the wall between them.

His frustration boiled over. He slapped the brass bedpost so hard it squeaked. "Dammit, Katrina, I'm trying to tell you I love you."

She turned, giving a sharp, strangled cry. He saw why she'd kept her back toward him. Her cheeks were wet with tears.

"Oh, Kitten. My poor darling." He circled the bed and took her in his arms, holding her with infinite care. Her body was so brittle he was half-afraid she'd break at his touch. Gently he brushed the tears from her cheeks. "I can't stand seeing you hurt like this and knowing I'm responsible. Can you forgive me? Will you believe me when I tell you I love you?"

She swallowed, her eyes bright with tears and misery. "How can I be sure? How do I know this isn't just another lie?"

He ran his thumb down the sensitive pulse at the side of her neck. "Trust your heart," he whispered huskily.

"My heart's been wrong before."

He lifted her hand and placed it against his wildly pounding heart. "Then trust mine."

Her palm pressed against him, its slight pressure turning his blood to fire. He wanted to crush her to him, to take her in a hundred different, pleasurable ways, to teach her to need him as completely as he needed her. Yet he waited, knowing she had to make the first move. Take her now and he'd have her body. But he wanted her heart.

Gently, almost unconsciously, she slid her hand across his chest, exploring the taut muscles beneath his dark shirt. He gritted his teeth and endured the sweet torture, until her light fingertips skimmed over his nipple. Desire ripped through him as he gasped aloud. "Kitten," he breathed, "give me a break. I'm dying here."

She looked at him, frankly startled that her innocent touch had caused such an explosive reaction in him. Then she glanced down to his abdomen and saw the evidence of his awakening desire. She raised her eyes, her smile peeping out like the welcome sun after a gray and dismal storm. "It doesn't look like you're dying to me."

That did it. In less than a minute he had her on the bed, stripped down to the wisps of lace that passed for her undergarments. Somewhere in the frenzy she'd managed to take off his own clothes as well, he couldn't remember how. He pressed her down into the soft comforter and kissed her until she moaned for mercy. His mouth caressed her lips, her throat, and her shoulders, devouring her, pouring his love over every inch of her glorious body. Claiming her as his.

It was impossible to love her gently. Madness possessed him as he tasted her breast through her lace bra, feeling its nipple harden under his moist, teasing touch. She writhed beneath him, soft, kittenish sounds escaping her passion-ripe lips. "Please, Jack," she whispered frantically. "Oh, please . . ."

He reached down and slid off her pants, tossing them aside with the rest of their discarded clothing. He looked at her, amazed again at the perfection of her body, and glorying in the fact that she was his. Nagging voices whispered that he didn't deserve her love, and that he'd bring her nothing but grief, but he refused to listen. He needed her like he needed the air he breathed. More.

She opened herself to him, offering herself with an eagerness and trust he'd never found with any other woman. He poised himself over her, aching to possess her, but knowing that mere physical possession was no longer enough. "Say it, Kitten," he groaned, "I need to hear it. Tell me you love me, in spite of everything."

Her eyes brimmed with tears, but not from sorrow. She reached up and traced the granite line of his cheek, gentling it with her touch. "I'll love you till the day I die, Jack Fagen."

Her words dissolved into a gasp as he entered her, merging their bodies into one. Once again the primitive heat consumed her, but love made it burn brighter, hotter. Katrina cried his name, destroyed and reborn in the glory of his loving. Heat and love raged through her like a series of stars exploding, until a last final nova burst through her with the heat of a thousand suns.

Later, much later she lay cradled against his chest, hearing him murmur words of praise and passion as he nuzzled her tousled hair. The joy of their loving lingered in her like the remains of a beautiful dream, gossamer and fire, too soon gone. She savored the memory, automatically storing it against the day when she'd have nothing left of him

but her memories. Unconsciously her arms tightened.

He sensed the change. "Kitten? What's wrong?"

I won't spoil his moment with my selfishness. "Nothing's wrong. It's just so . . . dark."

His chest rumbled with rich, warm laughter. "It
usually gets that way when the sun goes down."

She glanced at her window and saw the bright
stars. She turned her head, rubbing her cheek in the
musky heat of his chest, and looked up at him. "I
guess I didn't notice," she said, smiling.

"I guess not," he answered, smiling in return.

Starlight pooled in his eyes. Dark and light, he
seemed half-demon, half-angel. He was a man of
unfathomable mysteries, hidden passions, and profound contradictions. She knew it was neither safe
nor sane to love him, but love him she did. She loved
the whole of him, the devil and the saint.

A deep, entirely different rumble sounded in his
chest.

Kat's practical nature took over. "You're hungry," she said, and rose to sit beside him. "I'll make
us some dinner. Or," she added, her eyes sparkling
mischievously, "is it breakfast?"

"It's still dinner," he said, but there was no
answering smile in his words. "Kat, darling, I can't
stay. I have to leave."

Her throat tightened. She knew he had to leave

sometime, but she thought they'd at least have this night together. "So soon?"

"There's some people I have to see, people who need the information we found to ferret out the high-placed traitors. I was planning to leave as soon as we discovered the bank name, but—" He stopped, apparently sensing the stillness in her. He reached out his hand and caressed her cheek. "I won't be gone long, Kitten. Only for a few days."

Days? They'd only had a few hours together, a few precious minutes. Kat bit her lip to keep it from quivering. It wasn't fair to lose him so soon after they'd found love. It wasn't fair. "Where are you going?" she asked.

"Depends on where they are," Jack said, a trace of his humor returning. "Like me, they tend to live out of their suitcases."

Like him, she thought bleakly. She turned away, afraid that even the faint half-light would reveal the anguish in her expression. "Well," she said with forced brightness, "I guess I'll have to make your meal 'to go.'"

"There is something else you could do for me."

He dropped his hand and shifted himself to face her. Inches away, she could feel his masculine heat and smell the intoxicating musk of his skin. Being near him blew every fail-safe switch in her body.

"Name it," she said, knowing she'd willingly give him the world if he wanted it.

"I wouldn't ask you unless I really needed it," he said, sounding strangely unsure.

His vulnerability touched the deepest part of her. "Name it," she repeated softly. "I love you. I want to help. What do you need?"

He sighed and raked his fingers through his thick mane of hair. "What I need, Kitten, is your password."

NINE

Six days, Katrina thought, staring at her desk calendar. Nearly a week gone by and not a word from him. Not a phone call, not a letter. Not even a postcard. True, he'd warned her that he might not be able to contact her because he didn't know whether the hacker was monitoring her phone calls and her mail. That didn't stop her from worrying.

She pressed down the switch on her intercom. "Jenny, are you absolutely sure there's no more mail for me?"

"I went down to the mail room myself," her secretary answered. "I'd go down again, but they're closed now. It's after six."

Kat glanced at her watch. She hadn't realized it was so late. In her worried state of mind she'd forgotten all about the time . . . and her secretary. "Jenny, you should have gone home an hour ago."

"I know, Ms. Sheffield, but I wanted to be around if . . . well, if you needed me or something. I wanted to help."

"You just did," Katrina said, smiling softly. Jenny was more aware than anyone of how troubled Kat had been during this past week. The young woman's genuine concern meant more to Kat than she could say. "Go on home, Jenny. I'll be fine."

"All right," Jenny answered, sounding reluctant. "Oh, I almost forgot. Leonard wants to talk with you. He has those readouts on 'screw cap' tolerance statistics Marketing asked you for."

Kat rubbed her temples, trying unsuccessfully to relieve the pressure behind her eyes. *I'm falling apart at the seams, and Marketing wants me to think about building the perfect toothpaste tube.* She'd think it was funny if she didn't feel so awful.

Well, she simply wasn't up to discussing the future of world dental hygiene tonight. Sighing, she depressed the button on the intercom. "Jenny, tell Leonard I've gone home, and that he should go home too. I'll discuss the readouts with him in the morning. Good night."

She snapped off the intercom and rested her elbows on her desk, careful not to disturb the large pile of problem reports overflowing from her "in" basket. It had not been a good day. Every time she looked around, there seemed to be a new system fire to fight, or a new argument between two programmers to settle. Add to that her worries about Jack . . .

Sighing, she crossed her arms on her desk and laid her head down on top of them. The weariness she'd been fighting off all day seeped into her mind like water into the bottom of a sinking ship. *Good analogy*, she thought glumly, especially since she felt as if she were drowning in a sea of fear and uncertainty.

Jack, where in the hell are you?

Every passing moment brought some new dread. Was he safe? Was he hurt? Had the hacker's superiors caught up with him and made sure he'd never tell anyone about their covert operation? The sensible side of her nature reminded her that Jack was a professional, and that she was worrying for nothing. For a whole minute she felt better. Then she remembered Jack's precarious life-style, and his dangerous disregard for his own safety. Fear, quick and sharp, stabbed through her. If anything happened to him . . .

"Argh!" she cried, jumping up from her desk and starting to pace the floor. She hated, hated, hated this feeling of helplessness, this not knowing. Half of her wanted to knock Jack's block off for not finding some way to get in touch with her. Half of her wanted to wrap her arms around him and never let go.

"Hey, babe, what's shakin'?"

Katrina stopped pacing. She looked over to Einstein's console and saw that the red light on his video camera had switched on. Apparently Jenny wasn't the only one who'd noticed her troubled state of mind.

Kat was touched by E's concern, but she wasn't up to explaining her less than logical emotions to the computer. "Nothing's shaking, Einstein. Didn't you have some solar-energy modeling studies to finish?"

"Did. Modeling easy since Jack fine-tuned system. He's awesome."

E's obvious hero worship made her heart ache for Jack even more. She walked over to the beige leather couch in the corner of her office and sank wearily onto its cushions.

Einstein's camera lens whirred in for a tighter focus. "Something wrong, babe?"

"No," she said quickly. Einstein was too perceptive by half. "Er, what's PINK up to? Shouldn't you be keeping an eye on her?"

"Unnecessary. Since Jack taught her about OTB, she phones in bets. He's—"

"Awesome. I know," Kat said tersely. "Jack, Jack, Jack. Can't you talk about anyone else?"

"Affirmative," Einstein answered softly, "but wish you had told me limitation parameters before engaging in conversation."

Oh damn, she thought. She left the couch and walked over to the console. "I'm sorry," she said, patting the side of Einstein's VGA monitor. "Believe me, the last thing I want to do is hurt your feelings. I'm just . . . well, I might as well tell you. I'm worried about Jack. I haven't heard from him since he left. I don't know if he's okay, or where he is, or—"

"Denver," Einstein stated.

"Excuse me?"

"Denver," E repeated. "That's where Jack is, or where was yesterday. And before that Montreal, and New York, and—"

"Hold on a minute!" Katrina interrupted. "How do you know all this?"

"Because Jack's been entering programs into system core."

Kat looked at Einstein's speaker, wondering if she'd heard him correctly. "You mean, he's been keeping in touch with you, but not with me?"

"Not 'in touch,'" Einstein explained. "Cities mentioned were origin point for programs. Assumed you knew where he was since he's using your password to enter programs."

Her password. She'd given it to Jack that night, sure in the knowledge of his love. He'd told her he wanted to use it to investigate her system to help find the hacker, not to enter new programs into the secured core area. She frowned, surprised and a little disturbed by this new information. "What kind of programs is he putting in?"

"Don't know. They're read-protected. But why ask? Jack wouldn't do anything to hurt system, would he?"

"Of course not," Kat stated. Yet even as she said it uncertainty coiled through her. She loved Jack with all her heart, but could she trust him?

Doubts crept into her mind—doubts her security-trained mind couldn't help but examine. She'd been taught to look at the facts from all angles, including the disturbing ones. And what she was currently thinking about Jack was very disturbing indeed.

Fact: He'd fine-tuned her system, but the number of problems her programmers reported had almost doubled since he'd arrived. Fact: He'd told her he was working for the government, but she had no proof of it, or even the name of the department he was supposedly working for. Fact: He was entering secret programs into system core, using her password. . . .

Had she, once again, delivered her system into the hands of a handsome, deceitful opportunist?

"Kitten."

She whirled, startled by the unexpected voice. He stood near the door, where the fading light from her office window barely reached him. His dark polo shirt and darker slacks helped to gather the gloom around him, and for an instant she wondered if he was some figment of her confused mind, a man made of shadows.

Then Einstein stepped in, proving the specter's reality. "Jack! What's shakin'? How was your trip? Did you find the hacker? Did you—"

"Hey, one at a time. I'll answer all your questions, E," he said, laughing. Then he turned his eyes back to Katrina. "In good time."

Love and relief melted through her like sweet, hot honey. *He's safely home*, part of her mind chorused. *Run to him*. But even the heat of her love couldn't melt her cold uncertainties. She remained rooted to the floor, unable to move, almost unable to breathe from the unbearable weight of her warring emotions. "Uh . . . Hello, Jack."

A halfhearted hello wasn't exactly the greeting Jack had hoped for. Since their last night together he hadn't been able to get her out of his mind for a minute—for a second. A week away from her had been torture of the worst kind, worse by far than the long, grueling hours of travel and the longer waits between. He'd forgone at least two meals and the chance of a decent night's sleep to get back to her as soon as possible, to crush her against him and tell her how much he loved her. And all he'd gotten for his trouble was . . . Hello, Jack.

He didn't understand. They'd been everything to each other the night he'd left, or so he'd thought. Had she only pretended to care for him? Had she been lying when she'd told him she'd love him until the day she died?

No, he couldn't believe that. He wouldn't. There had to be another reason for her reserve, but he couldn't think of one. Unless . . .

"You know, don't you," he said, sighing.

Kat's eyes widened in surprise. "You're admitting it?"

"No reason not to, since you already know." He shook his head, looking for all the world like a tired, disheartened lion. "I wanted to tell you myself. How did you find out?"

"E told me," Kat whispered, shocked by his composure. Had he no conscience? He'd just admitted to sabotaging her system, just admitted to using her love—

"Einstein?" Jack's brows drew together in a puzzled frown. "How did he find out that I didn't catch the hacker?"

"You didn't catch the hacker?" she repeated hollowly.

"No, I didn't. My associates and I managed to

catch up with his superiors, but so far no one's talking." In a few easy strides he crossed the office and stood next to the console, stopping just short of touching her. He looked down at her, his eyes narrowed. "What did you think I meant?"

Standing this close to him, she could see the weariness in his eyes, the tension at the edge of his mouth. His clothes were rumpled and his hair looked like it hadn't seen a comb in days. His vulnerability shook her, undermining her resolve far more effectively than his strength or his potent physical presence. She clenched her hands to fists at her side, forcing herself not to reach up to soothe the tautness from his brow. She couldn't afford to. Not until she was sure. "I thought you meant the programs. The unauthorized ones you added to my system's core."

"They weren't unauthorized. You gave me your password."

Einstein chirped up. "He's right. Password guarantees authorization—"

"E, not now," Kat said, cutting off the computer midsentence. She turned back to Jack, her flashpoint temper sparking. "I gave you my password to trace the hacker, not to enter illegal, read-protected programs."

"They weren't illegal," he argued, his own temper rising. "And they were read-protected because I didn't want the hacker to know what was in them."

"Or me either, I suppose."

Jack swore. "This is great, just great. I move heaven and earth for you, and you do everything but call me an outright liar."

"And what about me?" Kat fumed. "How about what I went through? I stayed up nights worrying about you, wondering whether you were all right—"

"You did?"

She was too angry to notice the hushed surprise in his tone. "Yeah, and look what it got me. While I worried about you, you were going behind my back, adding illegal programs to—"

"They weren't illegal!" Jack sputtered, throwing up his hands in total frustration. "Dammit, Katrina, I'd leave this office right now if it weren't for one thing."

"And what would that be?"

"Your eyes," he said roughly. "You're ungodly beautiful when you're angry."

That stopped her. She stared at him, in open-mouthed surprise, apparently unable to think of a thing to say. Jack recognized an opportunity when he saw one. Before she could recover, he pulled her into his arms and covered her mouth with a deep, bone-melting kiss.

"No," she breathed, but her cry was lost in the

devouring heat of his caress. Blood roared in her ears, confusing her, thrilling her. Hands that should have pushed him away clutched at his shirt, pulling him closer. Lips that should have berated him moaned in ecstasy at his touch. Her mind might deny what they had together; her body never could. Dark or light, demon or angel, Jack Fagen was the man she loved.

When he finally lifted his head, she was spent and shaken, but it didn't matter. She was filled with the golden, singular peace she'd only found in his arms. She leaned against his broad chest and listened with pleasure to the galloping beat of his heart. "That wasn't fair," she said weakly.

His rich chuckle stirred her hair. "Oh, I'm way past fair." He tightened his arms around her, protecting and possessing her at once. "You were so distant when I walked in, Kitten. So cold. I thought I'd been wrong about what you felt for me. I had to know if you loved me."

"I love you," she told him. She sought out his hand, curling her small, subtle fingers around his blunt, powerful ones. "I'll always love you."

"But you don't trust me, do you?" he said quietly.

Her fingers involuntarily tightened around his. No, she didn't trust him, not entirely. He'd told her so many stories, she'd lost track of what was true and what wasn't. She loved him so hard, it ached her heart, but she didn't trust him. "Jack, I—"

Her words were interrupted by the whirring of Einstein's camera lens. "Excuse me."

Jack groaned. "Not now, E."

"Okay, I'll wait till later to tell you that someone's in the computer lab."

Katrina frowned, distracted from her own concerns by Einstein's comment. No one was scheduled to work in the computer lab tonight. She raised her eyes and saw that Jack was looking at E's console, his brow furrowed in concentration. The computer's comment had gotten his attention as well. "Einstein, who's in the lab?"

"Don't know. PINK and my video and audio feed's on the fritz. Body heat only indication of human presence."

Kat could understand if either E's video camera or audio pickup malfunctioned, but both of them going bad at once was too much of a coincidence. She automatically accessed the options and settled on the most likely: trouble. "Jack—"

"I'm with you, Kitten," he said, meeting her gaze with a ghost of his rakish smile. He gave her hand a quick, final squeeze before releasing her and heading for the door. "This may be the break we've been waiting for."

System-wise, maybe, she thought as she followed

him to the door. But, personally, she'd never felt less lucky. Jack's kiss still burned on her lips, but no amount of heat could burn away her distrust of him. God knows she wanted to believe he was being straight with her, but she couldn't deny that the facts were stacked pretty heavily against him.

She doubted if even the risk junkie PINK would take on those kinds of odds.

As Jack and Katrina stood in the middle of the bright, unnaturally quiet computer room, she tried not to shiver. Deserted, the place always gave her the creeps, and tonight was no exception. Machines clicked and whirred in the silence, following intricate instructions that left no room for human error and less room for human heart. She sidled closer to Jack's dark, unsilent, and eminently human form.

"Come on!" he bellowed for the second time in a minute. "We know you're in here. Where are you?"

Silence was his only answer. Kat scanned the banks and banks of equipment, trying to determine the most logical place for a person to hide. After a moment she pointed to the southwest quadrant of the room. "Let's start looking over th—"

Her last word was drowned out by the sound of something heavy crashing to the floor. Moving in tandem, she and Jack headed toward the sound.

They rounded a wall of CPU tower units and found—

"Leonard?" Kat said, surprised to see her assistant standing beside the little-used work station.

Leonard seemed as surprised to see them as they were to see him. "Why, hello, Ms. Sheffield, Mr. Fagen," he said as he righted the chair he'd apparently just tipped over. "What are you doing here?"

Kat opened her mouth to speak, but Jack was quicker. "I could ask you the same thing, Heep. Why didn't you answer when I called?"

"I must not have heard you," Leonard said, and waved his hand to indicate the portable CD player and earphones on his desk. "Up to a moment ago I was listening to Tchaikovsky."

Jack's eyes narrowed suspiciously. "You must have had the volume cranked up pretty high not to hear me."

"Jack!" Kat admonished. She knew Jack was naturally suspicious of everyone, but—Leonard? "We just didn't expect to find you here. You aren't scheduled to work this evening, are you?"

"Well, no," Leonard admitted. "I wanted to get some extra work done on those tube-tolerance figures before I discussed them with you." He smiled and looked at the floor, apparently embarrassed. "I wanted to surprise you."

Katrina smiled, touched by her assistant's dedication. After her doubts and uncertainties about Jack, it was nice to know that there were still people she could depend on. "That was very thoughtful of you, Leonard," she told him, "but I think you should go home and—"

"Mother of God," Jack said, interrupting her praise. Ignoring her dirty look, he pointed to the computer monitor on Leonard's desk. "Look. Look at the screen. It's the log-on."

Katrina did, but the display winked out before she could read it. She turned back to Jack, wondering what in the world he was talking about. "What log-on?"

"The log-on I saw the night of PINK's virus," he stated, running his hand quickly through his unkempt hair. He swung his gaze to Leonard and fixed him with the piercing stare of a hawk sighting its prey. "Leonard's the hacker who's been sabotaging the system."

"Leonard?" Kat said incredulously. Leonard was her right-hand man, and had been for years. He'd stood by her during her terrible time with Preston—there was no one she trusted more. She glanced at her assistant, thin and severe in his pristine lab coat, as homely and reliable as the computer hardware that surrounded him. He looked about as threatening as a toaster. "Jack, have you gone crazy?"

"On the contrary, Ms. Sheffield. He knows exactly what he's doing," Leonard said, his voice dropping to a conspiratorial whisper. "Think about it. We've had nothing but problems since he came here."

"I'll give you problems you never dreamed of, you little jerk," Jack growled as he took an ominous step toward Leonard.

"Now stop this," Kat said, automatically putting herself between them. Leonard was her assistant and she had to defend him, even if it meant facing down Jack's anger. Besides, considering Jack's size and strength, it would hardly be a fair fight. "Fighting won't get us anywhere."

"No, but it'll sure make me feel a helluva lot better," Jack argued. "Kat, this is the joker who's been messing with your system."

"He would say that," Leonard countered from behind the protection of Katrina's shoulder. "He blames everyone else, just like Preston Gates did."

Jack uttered a concise oath. "That does it. I'm taking you out now, buddy."

"No, you won't," Kat said, placing her hands on his chest and pushing him away. Too late she realized her mistake. Touching him, even in anger, was a drug to her senses. It brought too many memories to mind, memories that had nothing to do with Leonard, the hacker, or her computer system. Shaken, she looked up, and saw Jack staring down at her with all the uncertainty that she felt. His blue eyes, so quick to anger, now held an anguish so deep she felt she could drown in it.

"Kat, you don't actually believe this guy, do you?"

She swallowed, her throat suddenly tight with dryness. "I don't know what to believe," she said weakly. "But it's my system, Jack. I have to consider all the facts. If you were me, you'd do the same thing, wouldn't you?"

For a moment she thought he was going to argue with her. Then he shrugged his shoulders in a gesture that contained all the disappointment and despair he'd learned since he was a child. "Hell, Kitten," he said softly, "if I were you, I'd have booted my sorry hide out of here a long time ago."

And then she knew. The questions inside her stilled, dying like the last roll of thunder after a raging storm. She knew finally what really mattered. It wasn't what Jack did or said, or even what other people said about him. What mattered was Jack himself. She loved him—not with the shabby emotion she'd felt for Preston, but with a rich, burning purity that outshone the sun itself. She loved him enough to believe in him no matter what. Enough, even, to begin to believe in herself.

"Leonard," she said quietly. "What the hell have you been doing to my computer system?"

Leonard just stood there, his expression blank with shock. Then he pressed his mouth into a harsh, sinister line and Katrina caught a glimpse of the sly criminal lurking beneath his innocuous exterior—for an instant. Then he turned on his heel and sprinted like a scared rabbit out the door of the computer room.

"He's getting away," Kat cried, and started to follow.

Jack laid a restraining hand on her shoulder. "He won't get far," he promised. "Besides, there's something I want to show you. Look at the overhead monitor."

She looked up at the large monitor screen over the main console and saw, to her horror, what Leonard had really been doing in the lab. The virus was back with a vengeance, eating up her system core like there was no tomorrow. Apparently Leonard had disconnected the system alarm along with Einstein's external feeds. The virus had long since passed the point of no return. "No," she moaned, turning her face into Jack's shoulder.

"Wait," Jack told her. "Look again."

Reluctantly she looked back at the screen and saw that, unbelievable as it seemed, the computer virus was beginning to disintegrate. Like magic, the regions she'd feared were destroyed were purging the deadly intruder from their memories and returning to normal. She shook her head in amazement. "How . . . ?"

"My programs. The ones you were so worried about. They were designed to protect the system." He took her chin and gently tilted it up. "I may have disappeared, Kitten, but I never deserted you."

There was no condemnation in his gaze, only honesty and understanding, and a blue passion that melted through her like molten fire. "Oh, Jack," she began earnestly, "I'll never doubt you again. I'll—"

But before Katrina could finish her sentence, the door to the computer room was thrown open— loudly. People crowded into the lab—the expected security officers and night-shift operators as well as nearly a dozen new faces she'd never seen before. Everybody talked at once. They all collected around her and Jack like steel to a magnet, full of seemingly endless congratulations and questions.

Jack ignored both. He turned to the nearest stranger, a man with bulldog jowls and a head as bald as a bowling ball. "Did you get him?"

"'Course," the bulldog answered. "Got the others, didn't we?"

They're talking about Leonard, Katrina surmised. She couldn't grasp much else about the conversation. The evening's events had drained her of most of her strength, and the press of people was making her uncomfortably warm and light-headed.

Jack's laughter drew her back to the conversation. "Yes, this is the woman I wouldn't shut up about. Katrina, this is Mark Curtis, government watchdog."

"Gofer is more like it," Bulldog corrected. He offered his hand to Katrina. "Lady, if you're half as good as Fagen says you are, you can work with me anytime."

"Thank you," Kat said, or at least she tried to. She had trouble getting the words out. Her vision blurred. Bulldog's features ran together like a watercolor in the rain and the air around her felt stiflingly hot.

Jack's grip on her arm tightened. "Katrina?"

"She looks kind of pale," Curtis mentioned. "I think she's gonna faint."

"Nonsense," Kat stated, "I never faint. . . ." But even as she spoke, her knees gave out from under her and she sank to the floor. Jack's strong arms caught her up and drew her protectively against him. Cradled against the warm reality of his chest, she finally gave up her fight against exhaustion. And as the darkness enveloped her she thought absently that this fainting thing wasn't half so bad as everyone made it out to be.

TEN

The lamp on the table beside the office couch cast a pale circle of light on Katrina's already too-pale features. Jack settled on the couch beside her, resting his left arm across its back as he studied her face for some flicker of awareness. *Lord, Jack, you'd think you'd never seen anyone faint before.*

He tried to view this situation with the cold, clearheaded logic that had earned him his nickname. He failed miserably. This was Katrina, his Katrina, the woman who meant more to him than his own life. Her courage and strength amazed him. And her undeserved belief in him humbled him to his core.

She'd been in his thoughts every minute during the week he'd spent away from her. He'd stored up a hundred things he wanted to tell her, and a hundred ways to show her how much he loved her. On one particularly grueling stretch he even let himself imagine a shared future with her, a future where they could work together every day, and lie together every night. A happiness too rich for words filled him—for a moment. Then reality kicked in. He loved her too much to sentence her to this rootless existence. She deserved a secure life, full of kids and minivans and PTA meetings. She deserved a husband who could offer her more than a threadbare duffel bag and a dog-eared passport.

Katrina made a small sound and moved fitfully, but didn't wake. Worried, he circled her delicate wrist and felt for her pulse. The beat that drummed against his fingertips was reassuringly strong and steady. Still, by his estimation she should have come out of this faint by now.

Katrina had a lion's heart, but tonight she'd been tested to her limits. Loyalty meant everything to her, and even though that loyalty had been misplaced, he couldn't help but admire the way she'd stood up for Leonard. And then the little drip had gone and played her false. . . . Jack balled his fist, thinking that he'd have given just about anything to plant one on Heep's kisser.

If only he'd learned earlier that Leonard was the hacker—rules or not, he would have found some way to call and warn her, rather than springing it on her cold. Jack had seen tougher people than she was crack under far less pressure. He bent closer to her unconscious form and tenderly brushed the blond fringe from her forehead. *Mother of God, let her open her eyes*, he prayed, reverting to his old prayers. *Just let her open her eyes and I swear I'll never ask you for anything else. . . .*

Katrina opened her eyes. She blinked uncertainly, then a smile like sunrise spread across her face. "It wasn't a dream," she said softly. "You *are* back."

Jack gripped the edge of the couch, fighting a sharp, nearly uncontrollable need to take her beautiful body in his arms and assure her that he was most definitely *not* a dream. She needed patience right now, not passion. "I, er . . . how are you feeling?"

"Guess I'll live," she answered, still smiling. She rubbed the back of her hand across her eyes, then opened them and looked full at Jack. "Besides, I think I'm supposed to be angry with you."

Jack was so thankful to see fire in her eyes again, he didn't care if it was kindled by anger. "Why is that, Kitten?"

"Don't 'Kitten' me. You didn't tell me the building was crawling with federal agents. If I'd known, I wouldn't have been half so worried about you."

"I like having you worried about me," he said softly. He reached down and gently traced the delicate line of her jaw. "One of Leonard's superiors turned state's evidence in exchange for a lighter sentence. He didn't know the Sheffield hacker's name, but he did know that something was going down tonight. That's why Mark's people were all over the building."

A trace of uncertainty crept into her anger-bright eyes. "Jack, you didn't still think that I was the hacker, did you?"

"No," he stated roughly, dispelling her doubts. "I wanted to tell you about Mark's operation the moment I saw you, but I couldn't be sure the hacker hadn't bugged your office. I couldn't risk him listening in." He cupped her cheek, molding his fingers to her warm, yielding skin. "Forgive me?"

"I'll think about it," she murmured, but her irritation lacked its former conviction. Righteous anger was impossible to feel with Jack so close to her, feathering fire across her skin with his teasing touch. He was safe, and he was here. For six long days that was all she'd prayed for. She knew it was all she'd ever pray for.

It was crazy to want him this way, to care so much for a man as unreliable as the wind. But then, crazy had a lot to do with what had happened this evening. She felt as if she'd lived a lifetime of emotions in a few short hours: worry over Jack, Leonard's betrayal, the new virus—the virus! She pushed herself to a sitting position and looked at Jack, her eyes wide with worry. "What about Einstein and PINK? Are they okay?"

"Right as precipitation," Jack said, chuckling. "At least, that's how E put it after we hooked up his disconnected audio. As for PINK . . . the last time I saw her she was telling Mark all about trifectas and claiming races. Some things never change."

And never will, thought Kat, gazing into the eyes of the man she loved and would keep on loving until the breath left her body. The hard, haunted edge was gone from their blue depths, leaving a velvet peace behind. *I gave him that*, she thought proudly. And then, less triumphantly, she added, *He'll take that peace with him when he leaves*.

"Katrina, is something wrong?"

"It's just that so much has happened," she said, hoping the half-truth would suffice. "It's over, isn't it? It's really over?"

"Yes," he promised. He took her hand, lacing his larger fingers reassuringly through her own. "Leonard and his buddies will never bother you again."

Her bright eyes lost some of their sparkle. "Leonard," she whispered, her voice edged with sorrow. "I still can't believe he's the hacker. He helped me build this system in the first place. Why did he do it, Jack?"

"Money. Power. The terrorists offered him plenty of both." His eyes took on the tough, weary cast of a man who's seen too much. "Believe me, men have done far worse for far less."

She felt his weariness, and longed to soothe the painful memories from his soul. He'd seen so much, yet he'd held to his integrity where a lesser man might have chosen differently. Those choices had cost him. She could see that in every chiseled line on his rugged face. Yet those lines, and the tough choices that had caused them, made her love him all the more.

"Kitten," he said huskily, "you keep looking at me like that and we won't make it out of this office tonight."

She smiled shyly. "Well, it's my office, isn't it?"

Dark copper curls framed an expression that would have made a pirate blush. "Good point," he said simply.

He didn't move. He just looked at her, his intense eyes absorbing her like a dark star absorbs light. She felt herself falling into his heat, his power, his raw and potent need for her. For her—for too-tall Katrina who'd always hidden her love light under a bushel—for her and no one else. It humbled her to think that she alone could give this hard yet tender man the loving he so desperately needed. They'd both been lonely for so long, but in the universe of his dark eyes she found her second self. Jack needed her fiery brand of loving as much as she needed his.

She leaned toward him in the semidarkness of the room, and burned.

The office door opened. Mark Curtis stepped in, his bald head bent as he studied the thick folder in his hand. "Good news, Jack. You won't have to worry about Heep or his cyber bomb anymore. Central just called and told me we have enough to hold them till doomsday. . . ."

Mark's words dwindled away to nothing as he lifted his head and caught sight of the two on the couch. His eyes went from Jack, to Katrina, to Jack again. "Uh, how about I come back later?"

"How about you come back tomorrow?" Jack said through gritted teeth. "Or maybe the day after?"

"Okay, T-man," Mark said, his wide grin showing little fear for Jack's anger. He walked back to the door and started to shut it behind him. "Ma'am, see that he gets a little sleep tonight. He's been up for two—"

"Out!" Jack said, rising from the couch. He got to the door just as Mark's smiling face disappeared behind it. Fuming, Jack snapped the lock shut. "That guy gives new meaning to the term 'bad timing.'"

"Jack?"

"I know, Kitten," he said as he came back to the couch. "Mark's worse than a mother hen when it

comes to the people he likes, and for some unfathomable reason he likes me—"

Katrina hardly heard his words. "Jack, what did
he mean about 'cyber bomb'?"

Hell, Jack thought, wincing internally. He'd
wanted to spare her this. For a moment he considered lying to her, for her sake, but knew he couldn't
do it. There had already been too many lies between
them. She deserved the truth, no matter how un-
pleasant. He sat back down beside her and gently
took her hand in his. "Heep figured we were closing
in on him, so he planted a cyber-bomb virus—a kind
of computer time bomb—in your system. He
planned to use it as a bargaining chip if he was
caught. The smaller virus that we stopped tonight
was designed both to cover up his tracks and spread
the virus through every part of Sheffield's worldwide
network. Financial, scientific, and military systems
around the globe could have been destroyed. It was
the most insidious piece of technological terrorism
I've ever seen, bar none."

Katrina didn't say a word. She just stared at him
with a blank, almost unearthly intensity. Worried,
Jack tightened his grip on her hand. "I know what's
going through your mind. You think you've been
taken again by a man you trusted. You think you
can't trust anyone, maybe not even me. Damn, I

should have pulverized that little cyber punk when I had the chance."

"Jack, that's not what I'm thinking," she said quietly. She raised her free hand and tenderly stroked his bearded cheek. "I hate what Preston and Leonard did to my system, but I don't hate myself for believing in them. They were the ones in the wrong, not me. It's not a sin to trust someone, or," she added softly, "to love someone."

For a long moment Jack just stared at her, stunned by her words. Katrina began to feel a little like a museum item on display, and didn't like it. Grimacing, she gave Jack's beard a playful tug. "Hey, T-man, I just told you I loved you. Aren't you going to do anything about it?"

Jack feigned seriousness. "I don't know. Mark did say I should get some sleep."

"Hmm, so he did," Kat remarked. She dropped her hand to his chest and started to unbutton his shirt. She pushed open his collar and placed a hot, moist kiss at the base of his neck. "If sleep's what you really want . . ." she murmured.

It wasn't. Jack eased her down against the cushions, knowing from experience just where to touch her to give her the most pleasure. Her soft, throaty laughter set his heart clattering in his chest. While she was still laughing he kissed her, breathing her joy into him. Her laughter turned to sweet, aching moans under his lips.

He moved over her and fitted her hips to his body, letting her feel his need for her, heightening her arousal through their clothes. He planned to drive her crazy before the night was through—a slow, steady crazy that would prove to her beyond any doubt how much he loved her. They had time now, at least for tonight. He'd spent too much time dreaming of this moment to rush it.

He brushed his lips across hers in a teasing kiss, enjoying her soft groan of anticipation. He moved his kisses lower, feasting on the sensitive skin of her neck and deciding the most provocative way to relieve her of her blouse. Then he spoke. "I meant it," he murmured against her skin.

"What?" Kat said, her tight breath making even that one word difficult.

"When I said that even I wouldn't trust me." Slowly he raised himself until he was over her, and looked down, a puzzled expression on his face. "Tell me, why did you?"

She reached up and twined her fingers through his shaggy hair. "I'd much rather show you," she said, pulling his mouth to hers.

"Just one more."

"No, PINK," Jack said as he opened the drawer

to his office desk. He sifted through the contents, making sure he'd cleaned out all of his personal belongings. "Besides, I set up that phone account for you at Hialeah over a week ago. You can call them up anytime you want. You don't need me to place your bets anymore."

"But want you to place them," PINK protested. Her speaker crackled with unusually erratic frequency variances. "Want you to stay."

Jack stopped his packing. He propped his knuckles on the desk and leaned toward the compact speaker box, smiling thoughtfully. "I can't stay. My next job is clear on the other side of the world and I have to be there in three days. We have to say good-bye."

"Will miss you," PINK said morosely. "Big time."

"Ditto," Jack answered, meaning it. During his time here he'd grown attached to the vivacious little computer. He'd grown attached to a lot of things.

He straightened and cleared his throat. "Well," he said brusquely as he closed the desk drawer, "I'd better get moving. Be good after I'm gone, will you?"

"Bet on it," PINK told him. "Know what?"

"What?" he said as he bent down to retrieve his duffel bag from the floor beside the desk.

"Good-byes are not pieces of toast," she stated, and signed off.

From the mouths of computer babes. He eased the bag's wide strap onto his shoulder and headed for the office door. He had one more stop to make before he left his job at Sheffield Industries behind. One more good-bye . . .

Last night they'd made love with a silent, almost desperate fury. Unable to voice the depth of his feelings for her, he'd shown them with every stroke, every touch, every fevered caress. He'd poured himself into loving her, and she'd returned his love in kind. No woman had ever given herself to him with the passionate honesty that Katrina had. They'd shared their most secret desires last night, shared everything, in fact, except for a single word—good-bye.

He entered Katrina's outer office. "Jenny," he said as he swung the duffel to the floor, "will you tell your boss I'd like to see her?"

"But she's not here," Jenny answered, apparently surprised he didn't know. "She called to say she'd be in later."

Later—after he'd gone. Sharp disappointment cut through him, but he knew he couldn't blame Katrina for not wanting to see him off. How could they trade an antiseptic office handshake and innocuous well-wishes after the glory they'd shared last night, and all the nights leading up to it? But strained as their meeting would be, he dearly wanted to see her again, to look into those hell-and-heaven eyes of hers and say one more time that he loved her—

Jenny's words interrupted his thoughts. "I know she'll be sorry she missed you. Maybe you'd like to leave her a note?"

Saying what? Thanks for the good times, see you around? Even the Terminator couldn't be so callous. He pressed his lips together in a hard, unforgiving line. "I don't think so."

Jenny's face fell. *Poor kid*, he thought, *she really hoped Kat and I would end up together. She's a hopeless romantic, just like her boss.* Softening, he reached over and tilted up her chin. "Listen, you take good care of Ms. Sheffield for me, all right?"

"Yes, I will," Jenny said eagerly, her bright smile restored. "I'll tell her you stopped by. But are you sure you wouldn't like to leave a message?"

Jack patted the pocket of his jeans, feeling the outline of the farewell gift he was going to give to Katrina. Somehow dropping off such a private item seemed even worse than leaving a note. He left it in his pocket and bent down to retrieve the duffel bag. "Just tell her good-bye for me," he said as he hoisted the bag onto his shoulder. "Just good-bye."

He left the building and went to the garage,

tossing his bag into the back of the rented sports coupe. He still had a good three hours to kill before his plane took off. He'd hoped to spend that time with Katrina. He supposed he could always wait for the flight in the airport lobby, but he'd be doing plenty of that in the next few days. Besides, he needed some fresh air. He needed to go somewhere where a man could breathe.

The thought decided him. He got into the car and drove to the seaside boardwalk where he'd gone to lunch with Katrina on his first day at Sheffield Industries. It was nearly deserted, for the sky was overcast and the wind off the water was unseasonably chilly. Jack leaned against the boardwalk railing, not minding the cold or the solitude. He felt a kinship with the gray sky and the vast, empty ocean. He'd been a loner before, and liked it. He'd like it again, once he got the memory of Katrina's warm smile out of his heart. *Once hell freezes over.*

Unexpectedly he heard a familiar voice. "Lord, watch over me, for the sea is so vast and my boat is so small."

He spun around. Katrina stood behind him, her hands stuffed down into the pockets of her white nylon jacket. "Hi," she said shyly.

Jack blinked in surprise. "What are you doing here?"

"I followed you. I was waiting outside the parking garage and saw your car leave. I wanted to talk to you before you . . ." She shrugged, a slight, helpless gesture. "Anyway, I followed you."

He caught the edge of despair in her voice. "Kat, I have to leave. I've got another job."

"I know, but I've been doing some thinking since last night. I know you have to leave. But I think," she said, dropping her voice to a whisper, "I think you should take me with you."

Once she started, words poured out of her like wine from a bottle. "We work well together—your friend Mark said so. I could help you with the basics, and you could train me in different security techniques. I could relay that information back to Sheffield to help them build newer and tighter security networks. Since you stopped PINK's excursions and Leonard's not around to stir up trouble, there's nothing for me to do on-site here anyway."

Her words stopped as suddenly as they'd started. She shifted uneasily on her feet and pushed back a strand of hair that had blown across her cheek. "Well, what do you think?"

"I think," Jack said slowly, "that you're the sweetest, most courageous, most decent woman I've ever met. What you just said means a lot to me—more than you know. But I can't let you make that kind of sacrifice. You deserve a man who can give you a stable home, a secure future—"

"We're back to Ward Cleaver," Kat said, grinning wryly.

Jack's brow darkened. "This isn't a joke. I told you once I'm a hard man living a hard life. That hasn't changed. I can't stand being in one place for more than a few weeks. Traveling's in my blood."

"I love traveling," Katrina said. She twisted a piece of blond hair around her finger and added, more softly this time, "I love you."

Jack laughed, his eyes as bleak as the gray ocean beyond. "You say that now. But what about next month, when you get tired of living out of a suitcase? What about next year, when a job takes me into the desert, or lands me in the middle of a sweltering, bug-infested jungle?" He turned around and stared out over the empty expanse of water. "What chance does love have against that?"

He heard her move behind him. He expected her to say she agreed with him and bid him a tearful good-bye. Instead he felt a sharp, jabbing pain in his upper arm.

"Hey," he said, nursing the spot where she'd punched him, "what was that for?"

"Because you deserved it," she answered, her whole body bristling with sudden, spitfire anger. "How dare you think I'd stop loving you because of . . . climate! I don't care whether it's forty below or a hundred and ten in the shade as long as I'm with you. You're worried about bugs and jungles . . . well, let me tell you, mister, that's nothing compared to the hell I'll face if you leave me behind."

She took a step toward the railing and pointed out at the dark, rolling water. "My boat's out there on that ocean, too, you know, and it's just as small and lonely as yours. When I met you, I thought I'd found a friend, someone who could make that emptiness a little less lonely. . . ." She sputtered, her eyes sparking with lavender fire. She clenched her hands into fists, then opened them in mute frustration. "Oh, you don't understand. Why do I even bother?"

She turned and stalked off down the pier, her feet stomping loudly against the wooden planks. Jack watched her go, rubbing the place where she'd hit him, and smiled in a soft, totally un-Terminator-like way. Katrina's words had hit home, but not in the way she'd intended. For the first time Jack realized there was something he could give to her, something not even a minivan full of Ward Cleaver clones could provide. He could give her himself, and all the special, loving things he felt for her. And he could accept the love she wanted so badly to give to him.

Jack had always prided himself on the ability to make crucial decisions under fire. He made one now. He caught up with her, his long-legged steps easily matching her strides. "I don't suppose it would do any good to say I'm sorry," he offered

"Not much," she agreed, but her steps slowed to a normal walking pace.

Jack rubbed his beard, choosing his next words carefully. "You know, a very smart computer once told me that the best way to get back into a lady's good graces was to ask her to marry me."

Katrina's steps slowed to a crawl. She cast a quick, furtive look in his direction, as if she didn't entirely believe his words. Hardly surprising, thought Jack, when he considered the men she'd put her faith in. Both Preston and Leonard had used her trusting nature to further their own corrupt ends. Who could blame her for doubting him, especially when he'd spent the last few minutes telling her why he *wasn't* going to take her with him? She needed proof.

He reached into his back pocket. "I don't have an engagement ring on me, but I hope you'll accept this instead." Slowly, almost reverently he slipped the newly repaired chain with the shell charm over her head. The shell settled over her heart like a promise, whiter than even the white jacket it lay against. He took her shoulders and turned her to face him. "I love you, Katrina Alexandria Sheffield. Will you marry me?"

She met his gaze, searching for cynical metallic

hardness she'd seen there so often before. Instead she saw only love, and a confidence so absolute it could only come from the depths of his soul. She wasn't sure how or why the change had occurred, but she knew it was real. She moistened her lips, suddenly gone dry. "I hope you're not planning to use this method of making up to a lady very often."

Jack's smile broadened into his familiar impossible grin. "Just once, Kitten," he promised.

Happiness flooded through her so violently, she was afraid she might burst. She laid her head against his chest and felt his powerful, infinitely gentle arms encircle her. "I love you, Jack Fagen. I'll marry you whenever and wherever you say. And I'll—"

But she never got the chance to finish her declaration of love. Unexpectedly Jack uttered a sharp oath and started down the boardwalk, pulling her after him. "We've got to get to the airport to make new plane reservations, and we haven't got much time. First we'll stop by your apartment for your passport—hey, do you have a passport?"

"Yes," Kat said, struggling to keep up with both his mental and physical pace. "I haven't used it in years, but I think it's still valid."

"Good, that's one less thing to worry about. Secondly you can pack some clothes for the trip, though personally," he added as his lips curved into a disreputable smile, "personally I don't think you'll be wearing much for the next few days."

"Jack!" she said, counterfeiting shock. "What would Sister Barbara say?"

"She'd say—oh, hell!"

"She's say 'oh, hell'?"

"No." He laughed. "It's just that I almost forgot about Sister Barbara. She'll have my hide if I don't introduce her to the woman I'm going to marry. We'll have to schedule an overnight stop in Chicago."

Still striding, his feet hit the gravel edge of the parking lot. Kat's car was over to his right, but he ignored it and pulled her straight toward his black sports coupe.

"Jack, my car. I can't just leave it here."

"Sure you can. We'll leave your keys at your apartment. Then we'll get Jenny or one of your other friends to pick up the keys and collect the car." He unlocked the passenger door and pulled it open, grinning confidently. "Trust me, Kitten. This is what I do best."

Yes, it was, she thought, feeling she'd been caught up in a whirlwind. Quick decisions were what Jack excelled at, a trait she could learn from, yet modify with her own more cautious approach. They'd bring out the best in each other, and while life with him was bound to be unsettling, even precarious, it would never be boring. Her mind flashed back to a scene from her youth when she and her mother had been running to catch a London bus. She couldn't recall if they'd caught it or not, but she could remember they'd been laughing while they ran.

Smiling, she slid into the passenger seat, letting Jack close the door behind her. She remembered the first time she'd sat here, when Jack had taken her to the boardwalk for lunch and told her about his less than reputable past. She remembered how he'd tried to pretend he was feeding her a line. *Once a scoundrel, always a scoundrel*, she thought as she clasped her fingers around her shell necklace. *My own personal scoundrel.*

But even as she settled back against the soft leather, a sudden thought dimmed her happiness. "Jack," she said as he got into the driver's seat beside her, "do you think Sister Barbara will like me?"

Jack laughed. "She'll love you as much as I do. You've got so many wonderful qualities. You're stubborn, bossy, opinionated, and you've got a wicked left jab."

"Thanks a lot," Kat said, shaking her blond curls in a huff. "Maybe you should sign me up for a prizefight."

He shook his head, fixing her with a steaming gaze so intense it took her breath away. "The only one you'll be fighting with for the next fifty or sixty years is me." His mouth turned up in a slow, devilish smile. "Want to chance it?"

"You bet I do," she breathed softly.

He looked at her, his blue eyes clear of the desperate shadows that had haunted them in the past. Love burned in them, love true and hot enough to melt the icy metal barriers he'd built around his heart. He leaned toward her and placed a gentle kiss of promise on her lips. "Deal," he whispered.

THE EDITOR'S CORNER

The heroines in September's LOVESWEPT novels have a secret dream of love and passion—and they find the answer to their wishes with FANTASY MEN! Whether he's a dangerous rogue, a dashing prince, or a lord of the jungle, he's a masterful hero who knows just the right moves that dazzle the senses, the teasing words that stoke white-hot desire, and the seductive caresses that promise ecstasy. He's the kind of man who can make a woman do anything, the only man who can fulfill her deepest longing. And the heroines find they'll risk all, even their hearts, to make their dreams come true with FANTASY MEN. . . .

Our first dream lover sizzles off the pages of Sandra Chastain's **THE MORNING AFTER**, LOVESWEPT #636. Razor Cody had come to Savannah seeking revenge on the man who'd destroyed his business, but instead he found a fairy-tale princess whose violet eyes and spun-gold hair made him yearn for what he'd never dared to hope would be his! Rachel Kimble told him she'd known he was coming and hinted of the treasure he'd find if he stayed, but she couldn't conceal her shocking desire for the mysterious stranger! Vowing to keep her safe from shadows that haunted her nights, Razor fought to heal Rachel's pain, as her gentle touch soothed his own. **THE MORNING AFTER** is Sandra Chastain at her finest.

Cindy Gerard invites you to take one last summer swim with her fantasy man in **DREAM TIDE**, LOVESWEPT #637. Patrick Ryan was heart-stoppingly gorgeous—all temptation and trouble in a pair of jeans. And Merry Clare Thomas was stunned to wake up in his arms . . . and in his bed! She'd taken refuge in her rental cottage, never expecting the tenant to return that night—or that he'd look exactly like the handsome wanderer of a hundred years ago who'd been making steamy love to her in her dreams every night for a week. Was it destiny or just coincidence that Pat called her his flame, his firebrand, just as her dream lover had? Overwhelmed by need, dazzled by passion, Merry responded with fierce pleasure to Pat's wildfire caresses, possessed by him in a magical enchantment that just couldn't be real. But Cindy's special touch is all too real in this tale of a fantasy come true.

TROUBLE IN PARADISE, LOVESWEPT #638, is another winner from one of LOVESWEPT's rising stars, Susan Connell. Just lying in a hammock, Reilly Anderson awakened desire potent enough to take her breath away, but Allison Richards fought her attraction to the bare-chested hunk who looked like he'd stepped out of an adventure movie! Gazing at the long-legged vision who insisted that he help her locate her missing brother-in-law, Reilly knew that trouble had arrived . . . the kind of trouble a man just had to taste! Reilly drew her into a paradise of pleasure, freeing her spirit with tender savagery and becoming her very own Tarzan, Lord of the Jungle. He swore he'd make her see she had filled his heart with joy and that he'd never let her go.

Linda Jenkins's fantasy is a **SECRET ADMIRER**, LOVESWEPT #639. An irresistible rascal, Jack was the golden prince of her secret girlhood fantasies, but Kary Lucas knew Jack Rowland could never be hers! Back then he'd always teased her about being the smartest girl in town—how could she believe the charming nomad with the bad-boy grin when he insisted he was home to stay at last? Jack infuriated her and made her ache with sensual longing. But when mysterious gifts began arriving, presents and notes that seemed to know her private passions, Kary was torn: tempted by the romance of her unknown knight, yet thrilled by the explosive heat of Jack's embraces, the insatiable need he aroused. Linda's fantasy man has just the right combination of dreamy mystery and thrilling reality to keep your nights on fire!

Terry Lawrence works her own unique LOVESWEPT magic with **DANCING ON THE EDGE**, LOVESWEPT #640. Stunt coordinator Greg Ford needed a woman to stand up to him, to shake him up, and Annie Oakley Cartwright decided she was just the brazen daredevil to do it! Something burned between them from the moment they met, made Annie want to rise to his challenge, to tempt the man who made her lips tingle just by looking. Annie trusted him with her body, ached to ease his sorrow with her rebel's heart. Once she'd reminded him life was a series of gambles, and love the biggest one of all, she could only hope he would dance with his spitfire as long as their music played. Terry's spectacular romance will send you looking for your own stuntman!

Leanne Banks has a regal fantasy man for you in **HIS ROYAL PLEASURE,** LOVESWEPT #641. Prince Alex swept into her peaceful life like a swashbuckling pirate, confidently expecting Katherine Kendall to let him spend a month at her island camp—never confessing the secret of his birth to the sweet and tender lady who made him want to break all the rules! He made her feel beautiful, made her dream of dancing in the dark and succumbing to forbidden kisses under a moonlit sky. Katherine wondered who he was, but Alex was an expert when it came to games lovers play, and he made her moan with ecstasy at his sizzling touch . . . until she learned his shocking secret. Leanne is at her steamy best with this sexy fantasy man.

Happy reading!

With warmest wishes,

Nita Taublib

Nita Taublib

Associate Publisher

P.S. On the next pages is a preview of the Bantam titles on sale *now* at your favorite bookstore.

Don't miss these exciting books by your
favorite Bantam authors

On sale in July:
FANTA C
by Sandra Brown

CRY WOLF
by Tami Hoag

*TWICE IN A
LIFETIME*
by Christy Cohen

THE TESTIMONY
by Sharon and Tom Curtis

And in hardcover from Doubleday
STRANGER IN MY ARMS
by R. J. Kaiser

From *New York Times*
Bestselling Author

Sandra Brown
Fanta C

The bestselling author of Temperatures Rising *and* French Silk, *Sandra Brown has created a sensation with her contemporary novels. Now, in this classic novel she offers a tender, funny, and deeply sensual story about a woman caught between the needs of her children, her career, and her own passionate heart.*

Elizabeth Burke's days are filled with the business of running an elegant boutique and caring for her two small children. But her nights are long and empty since the death of her husband two years before, and she spends them dreaming of the love and romance that might have been. Then Thad Randolph steps into her life—a man right out of her most intimate fantasies.

Elizabeth doesn't believe in fairy tales, and she knows all too well that happy endings happen only in books. Now she wishes she could convince herself that friendship is all she wants from Thad. But the day will come when she'll finally have to make a choice—to remain forever true to her memories or to let go of the past and risk loving once more.

Cry Wolf
by
Tami Hoag

author of *Still Waters* and *Lucky's Lady*

Tami Hoag is one of today's premier writers of romantic suspense. Publisher's Weekly *calls her "a master of the genre" for her powerful combination of gripping suspense and sizzling passion. Now from the incredibly talented author of* Sarah's Sin, Lucky's Lady, *and* Still Waters *comes* Cry Wolf, *her most dangerously thrilling novel yet. . . .*

All attorney Laurel Chandler wanted was a place to hide, to escape the painful memories of a case that had destroyed her career, her marriage, and nearly her life. But coming home to the peaceful, tree-lined streets of her old hometown won't give Laurel the serenity she craves. For in the sultry heat of a Louisiana summer, she'll find herself pursued by Jack Boudreaux, a gorgeous stranger whose carefree smile hides a private torment . . . and by a murderer who enjoys the hunt as much as the kill.

In the following scene, Laurel is outside of Frenchie's, a local hangout, when she realizes she's unable to drive the car she borrowed. When Jack offers to drive her home, she has no alternative but to accept.

"Women shouldn't accept rides from men they barely know," she said, easing herself down in the bucket seat, her gaze fixed on Jack.

"What?" he asked, splaying a hand across his bare chest, the picture of hurt innocence. "You think *I'm* the Bayou Strangler? Oh, man . . ."

"You could be the man."

"What makes you think it's a man? Could be a woman."

"Could be, but not likely. Serial killers tend to be white males in their thirties."

He grinned wickedly, eyes dancing. "Well, I fit that bill, I guess, but I don't have to kill ladies to get what I want, angel."

He leaned into her space, one hand sliding across the back of her seat, the other edging along the dash, corralling her. Laurel's heart kicked into overdrive as he came closer, though fear was not the dominant emotion. It should have been, but it wasn't.

That strange sense of desire and anticipation crept along her nerves. If she leaned forward, he would kiss her. She could see the promise in his eyes and felt something wild and reckless and completely foreign to her rise up in answer, pushing her to close the distance, to take the chance. His eyes dared her, his mouth lured—masculine, sexy, lips slightly parted in invitation. What fear she felt was of herself, of this attraction she didn't want.

"It's power, not passion," she whispered, barely able to find her voice at all.

Jack blinked. The spell was broken. "What?"

"They kill for power. Exerting power over other human beings gives them a sense of omnipotence . . . among other things."

He sat back and fired the 'Vette's engine, his brows drawn as he contemplated what she'd said. "So, why are you going with me?"

"Because there are a dozen witnesses standing on the gallery who saw me get in the car with you. You'd be the last person seen with me alive, which would automatically make you a suspect. Patrons in the bar will testify that I spurned your advances. That's motive. If you were the killer, you'd be pretty stupid to take me away from here and kill me, and if this killer was stupid, someone would have caught him by now."

He scowled as he put the car in gear. "And here I thought you'd say it was my charm and good looks."

"Charming men don't impress me," she said flatly, buckling her seat belt.

Then what does? Jack wondered as he guided the car slowly out of the parking lot. A sharp mind, a man of principles? He had one, but wasn't the other. Not that it mattered. He wasn't interested in Laurel Chandler. She would be too much trouble. And she was too uptight to go for a man who spent most of his waking hours at Frenchie's—unlike her sister, who went for any man who could get it up. Night and day, those two. He couldn't help wondering why.

The Chandler sisters had been raised to be belles. Too good for the likes of him, ol' Blackie would have said. Too good for a no-good coonass piece of trash. He glanced across at Laurel, who sat with her hands folded and her glasses perched on her slim little nose and thought the old man would have been right. She was prim and proper, Miss Law and Order, full of morals and high ideals and upstanding qualities . . . and fire . . . and pain . . . and secrets in her eyes. . . .

"Was I to gather from that conversation with T-Grace that you used to be an attorney?" she asked as they turned onto Dumas and headed back toward downtown.

He smiled, though it held no real amusement, only cynicism. "Sugar, 'attorney' is too polite a word for what I used to be. I was a corporate shark for Tristar Chemical."

Laurel tried to reconcile the traditional three-piece-suit corporate image with the man who sat across from her, a baseball cap jammed down backward on his head, his Hawaiian shirt hanging open to reveal the hard, tanned body of a light heavyweight boxer. "What happened?"

What happened? A simple question as loaded as a shotgun that had been primed and pumped. What happened? He had succeeded. He had set out to prove to his old man that he could do something, be something, make big money. It hadn't mattered that Blackie was long dead and gone to hell.

The old man's ghost had driven him. He had succeeded, and in the end he had lost everything.

"I turned on 'em," he said, skipping the heart of the story. The pain he endured still on Evie's behalf was his own private hell. He didn't share it with anyone. *Rogue Lawyer.* I think they're gonna make it into a TV movie one of these days."

"What do you mean, you turned on them?"

"I mean, I unraveled the knots I'd tied for them in the paper trail that divorced them from the highly illegal activities of shipping and dumping hazardous waste," he explained, not entirely sure why he was telling her. Most of the time when people asked, he just blew it off, made a joke, and changed the subject. "The Feds took a dim view of the company. The company gave me the ax, and the Bar Association kicked my ass out."

"You were disbarred for revealing illegal, potentially dangerous activities to the federal government?" Laurel said, incredulous. "But that's—"

"The way it is, sweetheart," he growled, slowing the 'Vette as the one and only stop light in Bayou Breaux turned red. He rested his hand on the stick shift and gave Laurel a hard look. "Don' make me out to be a hero, sugar. I'm nobody's saint. I lost it," he said bitterly. "I crashed and burned. I went down in a ball of flame, and I took the company with me. I had my reasons, and none of them had anything to do with such noble causes as the protection of the environment."

"But—"

"'But,' you're thinking now, 'mebbe this Jack, he isn't such a bad guy after all,' yes?" His look turned sly, speculative. He chuckled as she frowned. She didn't want to think he could read her so easily. If they'd been playing poker, he would have cleaned out her pockets.

"Well, you're wrong, angel," he murmured darkly, his mouth twisting with bitter amusement as her blue eyes widened. "I'm as bad as they come." Then he flashed his famous grin, dimples biting into his cheeks. "But I'm a helluva good time."

Twice in a Lifetime
by
Christy Cohen

author of *Private Scandals*

Fifteen years ago, an act of betrayal tore four best friends apart . . .

SARAH. *A lonely newlywed in a new town, she was thrilled when Annabel came into her life. Suddenly Sarah had someone to talk to and the best part was that her husband seemed to like Annabel too.*

JESSE. *With his sexy good looks and dangerous aura, he could have had any woman. But he'd chosen sweet, innocent Sarah, who touched not only his body but his soul. So why couldn't Jesse stop dreaming of his wife's best friend?*

ANNABEL. *Beautiful, desirable, and enigmatic, she yearned for something more exciting than being a wife and mother. And nothing was more exciting than making a man like Jesse want her.*

PATRICK. *Strong and tender, this brilliant scientist learned that the only way to keep Annabel his wife was to turn a blind eye—until the day came when he couldn't pretend anymore.*

In the following scene, Jesse and Annabel feel trapped at a

*birthday party that Sarah is hosting and they have to escape
into the surrounding neighborhood.*

As they walked through the neighborhood of newer
homes, Jesse's arm was around her. He could feel every
curve of her. Her breast was pressed against his chest. Her
leg brushed his as she walked.

"Sarah's probably pissed," he said.

Annabel laughed. "She'll get over it. Besides, Patrick the
knight will save her."

Jesse looked at her.

"Have you noticed they've been talking to each other a
lot?"

"Of course. Patrick calls her from work. And sometimes
at night. He's too honest not to tell me."

When Annabel pressed herself closer to Jesse, he lowered
his hand a little on her shoulder. An inch or two farther down
and he would be able to touch the silky skin of her breast.

"Do you love him?" he asked.

Annabel stopped suddenly and Jesse dropped his hand.
She turned to stare at him.

"What do you think?"

With her eyes challenging him, Jesse took a step closer.

"I think you don't give a fuck about him. Maybe you did
when you married him, but it didn't last long. Now it's me
you're after."

Annabel tossed back her black hair, laughing.

"God, what an ego. You think a little harmless flirting
means I'm hot for you. No wonder Sarah needed a change of
pace."

Jesse grabbed her face in one hand and squeezed. He
watched tears come to her eyes as he increased the pressure
on her jaw, but she didn't cry out.

"Sarah did not cheat on me," he said. "You got the story
wrong."

He pushed her away and started walking back toward the
house. Annabel took a deep breath, then came after him.

"What Sarah did or didn't do isn't the point," she said
when she reached him. "She's not the one who's unhappy."

Jesse glanced at her, but kept walking.

"You're saying I am?"

"It's obvious, Jesse. Little Miss Perfect Sarah isn't all that exciting. Especially for a man like you. I'll bet that's why you have to ride your Harley all the time. To replace all the passion you gave up when you married her."

Jesse looked up over the houses, to Mt. Rainier in the distance.

"I sold the bike," he said. "Two weeks ago."

"My God, why?"

Jesse stopped again.

"Because Sarah asked me to. And because, no matter what you think, I love her."

They stared at each other for a long time. The wind was cool and Jesse watched gooseflesh prickle Annabel's skin. He didn't know whom he was trying to convince more, Annabel or himself.

"I think we should go back," Jesse said.

Annabel nodded. "Of course. You certainly don't want to make little Sarah mad. You've got to be the dutiful husband. If Sarah says sell your bike, you sell your bike. If she wants you to entertain twelve kids like a clown, then you do it. If—"

Jesse grabbed her, only intending to shut her up. But when he looked down at her, he knew she had won. She had been whittling away at him from the very beginning. She had made him doubt himself, and Sarah, and everything he thought he should be. He grabbed her hair and tilted her head back. She slid her hands up around his neck. Her fingers were cool and silky.

Later, he would look back and try to convince himself that she was the one who initiated the kiss, that she pulled his head down and pressed her red lips to his. Maybe she initiated it, maybe he did. All he knew was that he was finally touching her, kissing her, his tongue was in her mouth and it felt better than he'd ever imagined.

The Testimony

A classic romance by

Sharon & Tom Curtis

bestselling authors of *The Golden Touch*

It had been so easy falling in love with Jesse Ludan . . . with his ready smile and laughing green eyes, his sensual body and clever journalist's mind. The day Christine became his wife was the happiest day of her life. But for the past six months, Jesse's idealism has kept him in prison. And now he's coming home a hero . . . and a stranger.

In the following scene Jesse and Christine are alone in the toolshed behind her house only hours after Jesse's return . . .

"Jess?" Her blue eyes had grown solemn.

"What, love?"

"I don't know how to ask this . . . Jesse, I don't want to blast things out of you that you're not ready to talk about but I have to know . . ." An uncertain pause. "How much haven't you told me? Was prison . . . was it horrible?"

Was it horrible? she had asked him. There she stood in her silk knit sweater, her Gucci shoes, and one of the expensive skirts she wore that clung, but never too tightly, to her slender thighs, asking him if prison was horrible. Her eyes were serious and bright with the fetching sincerity that seemed like such a poor defense against the darker aspects of life and that, paradoxically, always made him want to bare his soul to that uncalloused sanity. The soft taut skin over her nose and cheeks shone slightly in the highly filtered light, paling her freckles, giving a fragility to her face with its combined suggestion of sturdiness and sensitivity. He would have thought four years of marriage might have banished any unease he felt about what a sociologist would label the "class difference" of their backgrounds, yet looking at her now, he had never felt it more strongly.

There was a reel of fishing line in his right hand. Where had it come from? The window shelf. He let her thick curl slide from his fingers and walked slowly to the shelf, reaching up to replace the roll, letting the motion hide his face while he spoke.

"It was a little horrible." He leaned his back against the workbench, gripping the edge. Gently shifting the focus away from himself, he said, "Was it a little horrible here without me?"

"It was a lot horrible here without you." The admission seemed to relieve some of her tension. "Not that I'm proud of being so dependent on a man, mind you."

"Say three Our Fathers, two Hail Marys, and read six months of back issues of *Ms.* magazine. Go in peace, Daughter, and sin no more." He gestured a blessing. Then, putting a palm lightly over his own heart, he added, "I had the same thing. Desolation."

"You missed the daily dose of me?"

"I missed the daily dose of you."

Her toes turned inward, freckled fingers threaded anxiously together. The round chin dropped and she gazed at him from under her lashes, a mime of bashfulness.

"So here we are—alone at last," she breathed.

Sometimes mime was a game for Christine, sometimes a refuge. In college she had joined a small troupe that passed a hat in the city parks. To combat her shyness, she still used it, retreating as though to the anonymity of whiteface and costume.

He could feel the anxiety pent up in her. *Show me you're all right, Jesse.* Something elemental in his life seemed to hinge on his comforting her. He searched desperately for the self he had been before prison, trying to clone the person she would know and recognize and feel safe with.

"Alone, and in such romantic surroundings," he said, taking a step toward her. His heel touched a shovel blade, sending a shiver of reaction through the nervously perched lawn implements that lined the wall. Some interesting quirk of physics kept them upright except for one rake that came whacking to the floor at his feet. "Ah, the hazards of these secret liaisons! We've got to stop meeting like this—the gardener is beginning to suspect."

"The gardener I can handle, but when a man in his prime is nearly cut down by a rake . . ."

"A *dangerous* rake." His voice lowered. "This, my dear, is Milwaukee's most notorious rake. More women have surrendered their virtue to him than to the legions of Caesar." He lifted the rake tines upward and made it walk toward her, giving it a lascivious whisper. "Don't fight it, *cara*. Your body was made for love. With me you can experience the fullness of your womanhood."

She laughed at his notion of the things rakes say, garnered three years ago from a teasing thumb-through of a certain deliciously fat romance novel that she had meant to keep better hidden. Raising one hand dramatically to ward off the rake, she said, "Leaf me alone, lecher!"

The rake took an offended dip and marched back to the wall in a huff. "Reject me if you must," it said, in a wounded tone, "but must I endure a bad pun about my honorable profession? I thought women were supposed to love a rake," it added hopefully.

A smile hovered near the edge of her husband's mobile lips. Christine recognized a certain quality in it that made her heart beat harder. As his hands came lightly down on her shoulders, her lips parted without her will and her gaze traveled up to meet the shadow play of desire in his eyes.

"Some women prefer their very own husbands." There was a slight breathless quiver in her voice, and the throb of tightening pressure in her lungs.

"Hot damn. A compliment." Jesse let his thumbs slide down the front of her shoulders, rotating them with gentle sensuality over the soft flesh that lay above the rise of her breasts. She had begun to tremble under the sure movements of his fingers, and her slipping control brought back to him all the warm nights they had shared, the tangled sheets, the pungent musky air. He remembered the rosy flush of her upraised nipples and the way they felt on his lips. . . .

It had been so long, more than six months, since they had been together, six months since he had even seen a woman. He wondered if she realized that, or guessed how her nearness made his senses skyrocket. He wanted her to give up her body to him, to offer herself to him like an expanding breath for him to touch and taste and fill, to watch her bluebell eyes grow smoky with rapture. But though he drew her close so that he could feel the lovely fullness of her small breasts pressing into his ribs, he made no move to lower his hands or to take her lips. She seemed entrancingly clean, like a just-bathed child, and as pure. The damaged part of him came to her almost as a supplicant, unwhole before her wholesomeness. *Can I touch you, love? Tell me it's all right . . .*

She couldn't have heard his thoughts, or seen them, because he had learned too well to disguise them; yet her hands came to him like an answer, her fingers entwined behind his neck, pulling him toward her warm mouth. He took a breath as her lips skimmed over his and another much harder one as she stood on her toes to heighten the contact. Her tongue probed shyly at his lips and then forced an entrance, her body twisting slowly into his, a sinuous shock against his thighs.

He murmured something, random words of desire he couldn't remember as he said them; the pressure of her lips increased, and he felt thought begin to leave, and a growing pressure behind his eyelids. His hands were drifting over her blindly, as in a vision, until a shuddering fever ran through his veins and he dragged her close, pulling her hard into him, holding her there with one arm while the other slid under her sweater, his fingers spreading over the powdery softness of her skin. A surprised moan swept from her mouth into his lips as his hand lightly covered her breast. His palm absorbed her warmth, her delicate shape, and the thrillingly uneven pattern of her respiration before slipping to the fine heat and velvet distension of her nipple.

This time he heard his own whisper, telling her that he loved her, that she bewitched him, and then repeating her name again and again with the rhythm of his mouth and tongue. He was overcome, lost in her elemental femaleness, his pulse hammering through his body. Leaning her back, bringing his mouth hard against hers, he poured his kiss into her until their rapid breathing came together and he could feel every silken inch of her with the front of his body.

A keen breeze rattled the roof of the shed. It might have been the sound that brought him back, or perhaps some inner thermostat of his own, but he became aware suddenly that he was going to take her here in old man Jaroch's toolshed. And then he thought, Oh, Christ, how hard have I been holding her? His own muscles ached from the force, and he brought his head up to examine her upturned face. Sleepy lashes dusted her cheeks. A contented smile curved over damp and swollen lips. Her skin was lustrous. He pulled her into the curve of his arm with a relieved sigh, cradling her while he tried to contain his overwhelming appetite. Not here, Ludan. Not like this, with half your mind on freeze.

Kissing her once on each eyelid, he steeled his self-restraint and put her very gently from him. Her eyes flew open; her gaze leaped curiously to his.

"Heart of my heart, I'm sorry," he said softly, smiling at her, "but if I don't take my shameless hands off you . . ."

"I might end up experiencing the fullness of my woman-hood in a toolshed?" she finished for him. Her returning grin had a sexy sweetness that tested his resolution. "It's not the worst idea I've ever heard."

But it is, Chris, he thought. Because enough of me hasn't walked out of that cell yet to make what would happen between us into an act of love. And the trust I see in your eyes would never allow me to give you less.

CALL JAN SPILLER'S ASTROLINE

DAILY PERSONALIZED PREDICTIONS!

ONLY FORECAST OF ITS KIND!

This is totally different from any horoscope you've ever heard and is the most authentic astrology forecast available by phone! Gain insight into LOVE, MONEY, HEALTH, WORK.

Empower yourself with this amazing astrology forecast. Let our intuitive tarot readings reveal with uncanny insight your personal destiny and the destinies of those close to you.

Jan Spiller, one of the world's leading authorities in astrological prediction, is an AFA Faculty Member, author, full-time astrologer, speaker at astrology and healing conferences, an astrology columnist for national newspapers and magazines, and had her own radio astrology show.

1-900-903-8000 ★ ASTROLOGY FORECAST
1-900-903-9000 ★ TAROT READING

99¢ For The First Min. ★ $1.75 For Each Add'l. Min. ★ Average Length Of Call 7 Min.

CALL NOW AND FIND OUT WHAT THE STARS HAVE IN STORE FOR YOU TODAY!

Call 24 hours a day, 7 days a week. You must be 18 years or older to call and have a touch tone phone. Astral Marketing 1-702-251-1415.

DHS 7/93

OFFICIAL RULES

To enter the sweepstakes below carefully follow all instructions found elsewhere in this offer.

The **Winners Classic** will award prizes with the following approximate maximum values: 1 Grand Prize: $26,500 (or $25,000 cash alternate); 1 First Prize: $3,000; 5 Second Prizes: $400 each; 35 Third Prizes: $100 each; 1,000 Fourth Prizes: $7.50 each. Total maximum retail value of Winners Classic Sweepstakes is $42,500. Some presentations of this sweepstakes may contain individual entry numbers corresponding to one or more of the aforementioned prize levels. To determine the Winners, individual entry numbers will first be compared with the winning numbers preselected by computer. For winning numbers not returned, prizes will be awarded in random drawings from among all eligible entries received. Prize choices may be offered at various levels. If a winner chooses an automobile prize, all license and registration fees, taxes, destination charges and, other expenses not offered herein are the responsibility of the winner. If a winner chooses a trip, travel must be complete within one year from the time the prize is awarded. Minors must be accompanied by an adult. Travel companion(s) must also sign release of liability. Trips are subject to space and departure availability. Certain black-out dates may apply.

The following applies to the sweepstakes named above:

No purchase necessary. You can also enter the sweepstakes by sending your name and address to: P.O. Box 508, Gibbstown, N.J. 08027. Mail each entry separately. Sweepstakes begins 6/1/93. Entries must be received by 12/30/94. Not responsible for lost, late, damaged, misdirected, illegible or postage due mail. Mechanically reproduced entries are not eligible. All entries become property of the sponsor and will not be returned.

Prize Selection/Validations: Selection of winners will be conducted no later than 5:00 PM on January 28, 1995, by an independent judging organization whose decisions are final. Random drawings will be held at 1211 Avenue of the Americas, New York, N.Y. 10036. Entrants need not be present to win. Odds of winning are determined by total number of entries received. Circulation of this sweepstakes is estimated not to exceed 200 million. All prizes are guaranteed to be awarded and delivered to winners. Winners will be notified by mail and may be required to complete an affidavit of eligibility and release of liability which must be returned within 14 days of date on notification or alternate winners will be selected in a random drawing. Any prize notification letter or any prize returned to a participating sponsor, Bantam Doubleday Dell Publishing Group, Inc., its participating divisions or subsidiaries, or the independent judging organization as undeliverable will be awarded to an alternate winner. Prizes are not transferable. No substitution for prizes except as offered or as may be necessary due to unavailability, in which case a prize of equal or greater value will be awarded. Prizes will be awarded approximately 90 days after the drawing. All taxes are the sole responsibility of the winners. Entry constitutes permission (except where prohibited by law) to use winners' names, hometowns, and likenesses for publicity purposes without further or other compensation. Prizes won by minors will be awarded in the name of parent or legal guardian.

Participation: Sweepstakes open to residents of the United States and Canada, except for the province of Quebec. Sweepstakes sponsored by Bantam Doubleday Dell Publishing Group, Inc., (BDD), 1540 Broadway, New York, NY 10036. Versions of this sweepstakes with different graphics and prize choices will be offered in conjunction with various solicitations or promotions by different subsidiaries and divisions of BDD. Where applicable, winners will have their choice of any prize offered at level won. Employees of BDD, its divisions, subsidiaries, advertising agencies, independent judging organization, and their immediate family members are not eligible.

Canadian residents, in order to win, must first correctly answer a time limited arithmetical skill testing question. Void in Puerto Rico, Quebec and wherever prohibited or restricted by law. Subject to all federal, state, local and provincial laws and regulations. For a list of major prize winners (available after 1/29/95): send a self-addressed, stamped envelope entirely separate from your entry to: Sweepstakes Winners, P.O. Box 517, Gibbstown, NJ 08027. Requests must be received by 12/30/94. DO NOT SEND ANY OTHER CORRESPONDENCE TO THIS P.O. BOX.